COSMIC KILL

By
ROBERT SILVERBERG
(*originally writing as Robert Arnette*)

ARMCHAIR FICTION
PO Box 4369, Medford, Oregon 97504

*Our special thanks to
Robert Silverberg,
one of Science Fiction's best friends*

*For more information about Armchair Books and products, visit our
website at…*

www.armchairfiction.com

Or email us at…

armchairfiction@yahoo.com

A DEADLY GAME OF MARTIAN INTRIGUE

When Intelligence assigned Lon Archman to assassinate one of the most powerful men in the Solar System, Archman knew there was little chance of his coming back alive. The evil lord Darrien had established a foothold on Mars and was firmly in control of the Martian city, Canalopolis. Archman knew he'd have to land on Mars, enter Canalopolis, elude security, find his way into Darrien's palace, and then figure out who was the real Darrien, and not just one of several orthysynthetic robot doubles. No easy task! But with the arrival of two unexpected players—a beautiful Earth girl and a crafty Mercurian—Archman's task became more complicated than ever. Could he use these two new players to his advantage, or would they prove to be the harbingers of his death?

Join science fiction maestro Robert Silverberg for a funhouse ride in this nail-biting sequel to Paul W. Fairman's "Empire of Evil."

FOR A COMPLETE SECOND NOVEL, TURN TO PAGE 85

CAST OF CHARACTERS

LON ARCHMAN
He had a job to do, to kill one of the vilest creatures in the galaxy. But could he afford to let a pretty face get in his way?

ELISSA HALL
This beautiful nineteen-year old was the lead pawn in a deadly triangle that could determine the fate of the entire solar system.

HENDRIN
He came to the palace with a beautiful Earth girl in tow, a morsel for the mighty lord Darrien—but what was his real motive?

MERYOLA
As the aging mistress of the lord Darrien, she yielded great power…until the arrival of a beautiful young Earth girl.

DARRIEN
This wrinkled, shrunken man was the master of an empire of evil—and the would-be target of an assassin's zam-gun blast.

WENTWORTH
He'd been with Intelligence for a long time, so he was used to sending men out on missions that guaranteed their deaths.

DORVIS GRAAL
Darrien's Viceroy and the Chief of Canalopolis' Security Police, he was a crafty Venusian and Darrien's right-hand man.

.

FOREWORD

By Robert Silverberg

Cosmic Kill
(1957)

In the 1950s magazine covers were printed well ahead of the interiors of the magazines, done in batches of, I think, four at a time. This was a matter of economics—using one large plate to print four covers at once was much cheaper than printing them one by one. But sometimes the practice created problems.

For example, the April, 1957 cover of *Amazing Stories* was printed in the fall of 1956 with a group of others, well ahead of its publication date, bearing this announcement above the name of the magazine:

BEGINNING—COSMIC KILL—2-part serial of thundering impact

"Cosmic Kill" was supposed to be a sequel to a short novel that *Amazing* had published six years before— "Empire of Evil," by Robert Arnette. The readers had supposedly been clamoring for a follow-up to that great story all that time, and now, finally, it was going to be published.

The trouble was that the actual author behind the "Arnette" pseudonym on "Empire of Evil" was Paul W. Fairman, and Fairman, having recently become the editor of *Amazing* and *Fantastic,* suddenly found that he didn't have time to write a two-part serial of thundering impact. By December, 1956 publication day was nearing, though, for the April issue, due out in February, and a serial had to be found for it. So Paul Fairman phoned me one December morning and asked if I would mind very much writing a two-part serial called "Cosmic Kill," a sequel to something of his from 1951—and deliver it the following week, because it had to be on the newsstands two months from then.

Sure, I said. Nothing to it.

That night I dug out the January, 1951 *Amazing* and read "Empire of Evil," which turned out to be a wild and woolly thing starring blue Mercurians with green blood, savage Martian hill men that had nasty tusks, and Venusians with big black tails. Even back then we knew that there weren't any Mercurians, Martians, or Venusians, of course. That didn't really matter to me at the moment. What did matter was that I had to put together a story of some sort, more or less overnight, that was in some way connected to its predecessor, and Fairman had either killed off or married off nearly all the characters in the original piece.

Well, never mind that, either. He had left one or two surviving villains, and I invented a couple of new characters to set out after them, and in short order I had put together a plot. It wasn't going to be a literary masterpiece; it was just going to be a sequel, written to order, to Fairman's slapdash space-opera, which had been goofy to the point of incoherence. But—what the hell—no one was going to know I had written it, after all. And I reminded myself that plenty of my illustrious colleagues had written pulp-magazine extravaganzas just as goofy in their younger days. Here was my revered Henry Kuttner's novelet from *Marvel Science Stories* of 1939, "The Time Trap," with this contents-page description: "Unleashed atomic force hurled Kent Mason into civilization's dawn-era, to be wooed by the Silver Princess who'd journeyed from 2150 A.D., and to become the laboratory pawn of Greddar Klon—who'd been projected from five hundred centuries beyond Mason's time sector!" Kuttner had put his own name on that one. And here in the same issue was future Grand Master Jack Williamson with "The Dead Spot"—"With his sigma-field that speeded evolution to the limit imposed by actual destruction of germ cells, plus his technique of building synthetic life, Dr. Clyburt Hope set out to create a new race—and return America's golden harvest land into a gray cancer of leprous doom!"

The reputations of Kuttner and Williamson had survived their writing such silly stories. So would mine. But would I survive writing a 20,000-word novella in two days, which is what Fairman was expecting me to do?

Here my collaborator Randall Garrett came to my aid. I have never been much of a user of stimulants—I don't even drink coffee. Garrett, though, said that my predicament could be solved with the help of something called benzedrine—we would call it "speed," today— which he happened to take to control his weight. A little benzedrine would hop up my metabolism to the point where writing 40 pages in a one-day sitting would be no problem at all.

So he came over to my West End Avenue place and gave me a few little green pills, and the next day I wrote the first half of "Cosmic Kill," and the day after that I wrote the second half. I went out of my way to mimic the style of the original story, using all sorts of substitutes for "he said" that were never part of my own style—"he snapped," "he wheezed," "she wailed" and peppering the pages with adverbial modifiers—"he continued inexorably," "he said appreciatively," "he remarked casually." The next day I took the whole 80-page shebang down to Paul Fairman's office and it went straight to the printer. It was just in time for serialization in the April and May, 1957 issues of Amazing, my one and only appearance under the byline of Robert Arnette. And on the seventh day I rested, you betcha.

The funny thing is that "Cosmic Kill" isn't really so bad. I had to read it for the first time in 48 years for a recent Silverberg collection, and I was impressed with the way it zips swiftly along from one dire situation to another without pausing for breath, exactly as its author did back there in December, 1956. Treat it as the curio it is: the one and only example of Silverberg writing a story on speed.

CHAPTER ONE

LON ARCHMAN waited for the Martian to come nearer. Around him, whined the ancient world's hell-winds and Archman shivered involuntarily as he squeezed tighter on the butt of the zam-gun.

One shot left. And if the Martian were to fire before he did—

The wind picked up as he crouched behind the twisted gabron-weed. The Martian advanced steadily, its heavy body swung forward in a low crouch. It was still out of range of the zam-gun. Archman didn't dare fire yet—not with only one charge left.

A gust of devilish wind blew sand in the Earthman's face. He spat and dug at his eyes. An undercurrent of fear beat in the back of his mind. He shoved the emotion away. Fear and Lon Archman did not mix.

But where the blazes was that Martian?

Ah—there. Stooping now behind the clump of gabron-weed. Inching forward on his belly, Archman could see the hill-creature's tusks glinting in the dim light. His finger wavered on the zam-gun's trigger. Again a gust of wind tossed sand in his eyes.

That was the Martian's big advantage, he thought. A transparent eyelid that kept the damned sand out.

Well, I've got an advantage too. I'm an agent of Universal Intelligence, and that's just a dumb Martian hillman out there trying to kill me.

A torrent of sand swept down over them again. Archman fumbled on the desert floor and grabbed a heavy lichen-encrusted rock. He heaved it as far as he could—forty feet, in Mars' low grav. It kicked up a cloud of sand. Archman choked.

The Martian squealed in triumph and fired. Archman grinned, cupped his hands, threw his voice forty feet. The rock seemed to scream in mortal agony, ending in a choking gasp of death.

The Martian rose confidently from his hiding place to survey the smoking remains of Archman. The Earthman waited until the Martian's tusked head and shoulders were visible, then jammed down on the zam-gun's firing stud.

The Martian gasped as the force-beam hit him, and toppled slowly, his massive body burned to a hard black crust. Archman kept the beam on him until it flickered out, then thrust the now-useless zam-gun in his belt sash and stood up.

He took three steps forward on the crunching sand— and suddenly bleak Mars dissolved and he was back in the secret offices of Universal Intelligence, on Earth. He heard the wry voice of Blake Wentworth, *Chief of Intelligence,* saying, "The next time you fight on Mars, Archman, it'll be for keeps."

THE shock of transition numbed Archman for a second, but he bounced out of his freeze lightning-fast. Eyeing Wentworth he said, "You mean I passed your test?"

The Intelligence Chief toyed with his double chin, scowled, referred to the sheet of paper he held in his hand. "You did. You passed this test. But that doesn't mean you would have survived the same situation on Mars."

"How so?"

"After killing the Martian you rose without looking behind you. How did you know there wasn't another Martian back there waiting to pot you the second you stood up? You would have been a goner."

"Well, I—" Archman reddened, realizing he had no excuse. He had committed an inexcusable blunder. "I didn't know, Chief. I fouled up. I guess you'll have to look for someone else for the job of killing Darrien."

"Like hell I will! You're the man I want!"

"But—"

"You went through the series of test conflicts with 97.003 percent of success. The next best man in Intelligence scored 89.62. That's not good enough. We figured 95% would be the kind of score a man would need in order to get to Mars, find Darrien, and kill him. You exceeded that mark by better than two percent. As for your blunder at the end—well, it doesn't change things. It simply means you may not come back alive after the conclusion of your mission. But we don't worry about that in Intelligence, do we, Archman?"

"No, sir."

"Good. Let's get out of this testing lab, then, and into my office. I'll fill you in on the details. There are a lot of things you must know."

Wentworth led the way to an inner office and dropped down behind a desk specially contoured to admit his bulk. He mopped away sweat and stared at the waiting Archman.

"How much do you know about Darrien, Lon?"

"That he's an Earthman who hates Earth. That he's one of the System's most brilliant men—and its most brilliant criminal. He tried to overthrow the government twice, and the public screamed for his execution. But instead the High Council sent him to the penal colony on Venusia, in deference to his extraordinary mind."

"Yes," wheezed Wentworth. "The most disastrous move so far this century. I did my best to have that reptile executed, but the Council ignored me. So they sent him to Venusia—and in that cesspool he gathered a network of criminals around him and established his empire. An empire we succeeded in destroying thanks to the heroic work of Tanton."

Archman nodded solemnly. Everyone in Intelligence knew of Tanton, the semi-legendary blue Mercurian who had given his life to destroy Darrien's vile empire. "But Darrien escaped, sir. Even as *Space Fleet Three* was bombarding Venusia, he and his closest henchmen got away on gravplates and escaped to Mars."

"Yes," said Wentworth. "To Mars. Where in the past five years he's proceeded to establish a new empire twice as deadly and vicious as the one on Venus. We know he's gathering strength for an attack on Earth—for an attack on the planet that cast him out, on the planet he hates more than anything in the cosmos."

"Why don't we just send a fleet up there and blast him out the way we did the last time?" Archman asked.

"Three reasons. One is the Clanton Space Mine, the umbrella of force-rays that surrounds his den on Mars and makes it invulnerable to attack—"

"But Davison has worked out a nullifier to the Clanton Mine, sir! That's no reason—"

"Two," continued Wentworth, "even though we can break down his barrier, our hands are tied. Darrien has not done anything—*yet.* We know he's going to attack Earth with all he's got, any day or week or month now— as soon as he's ready. But until he does, we can't move. Earth doesn't fight preventive wars. We'd have a black eye with the whole galaxy if we declared war on Darrien after all our high-toned declarations."

"I suppose you're right."

"And Three. Intelligence doesn't like to make the same mistake a second time. We bombed Darrien once, and he got away. This time, we're going to make sure we get him."

"By sending me, you mean?"

"Yes. Your job is to infiltrate into Darrien's city, find him, and kill him. It won't be easy. We know Darrien has several doubles, orthysynthetic duplicate robots. You'll have to watch out for those. You won't get two chances to kill the real Darrien."

"I understand, sir."

"And one other thing—this whole expedition of yours is strictly unofficial and illegal."

"Sir?"

"You heard me. You won't be on Mars as a representative of Universal Intelligence. You're there on your own, as Lon Archman, Killer. Your job is to get Darrien without implicating Earth. Knock him off and the whole empire collapses.   You'll be on your own, Archman. And you probably won't come back."

"I understand, sir."

"Good. You leave for Mars tonight."

CHAPTER TWO

A PAIR of black-tailed Venusians were sitting at the bar with a white-skinned Earth girl between them, as Hendrin the Mercurian entered. He had been on Mars only an hour, and wanted a drink to warm his gullet before he went any further. This was a cold planet; despite his thick shell-like hide, Hendrin didn't overmuch care for the Martian weather.

"I'll have a double bizant," he snapped, spinning a silver three-creda piece on the counter. One of the Venusians looked up. The whip-like black tail twitched.

"You must have a powerful thirst, Mercurian."

Hendrin glanced at him scornfully. "I'm just warming up for some serious drinking, friend. Bizant sets the blood flowing; it's only a starter."

The drink arrived. He downed it in a quick gulp. That was good, he thought. "I'll have another…and a shot of dolbrouk for a chaser."

"That's more like it," said the Venusian. "You're a man after my own heart." To prove it, he downed his own drink—a mug of fiery brez. Roaring, he slapped his companion's back and pinched the arm of the silent Earthgirl.

Ideas started to form in Hendrin's mind. He was alone on a strange planet, and a big job faced him. These two Venusians were drunk and they wore the tight gray britches and red tunic of Darrien's brigades. That was good.

The girl was young and frightened; probably she'd been caught in a recent raiding-party. Her clothes hung in tatters revealing bare white thighs and the soft curve of her breasts. Maybe I can use the girl, Hendrin thought.

The Mercurian left his place at the bar and walked over to the carousing Venusians. "You sound like my type of men," he said. "Got some time?"

"All the time in the universe!"

"Good enough. Let's take a booth in the back and see how much good brew we can pour into ourselves," Hendrin jingled his pocket. "There's plenty of cash here—cash I'd part with for the company of two such as you."

The Venusians exchanged glances, which Hendrin did not miss. A sucker. "Come, wench," said one Venusian thickly. "Let's join this gentleman at a booth."

Hendrin jammed his bulk into one corner of the booth. One of the Venusians sat by his side. Across from him sat the other Venusian and the girl. Her eyes were red and raw, and her throat showed the mark of a recent rope.

Hendrin grinned. "Where'd you get the girl?"

"Planetoid Eleven," one of the Venusians told him. "We were on a raiding party for Darrien. Found her in one of the colonies. A nice one, eh!"

"I've seen better," remarked Hendrin casually. "She looks sullen."

"They all do. But they warm up. How about some drinks?"

Hendrin ordered a round of brez and tossed the barkeep another three-creda coin. The drinks arrived. The Venusian nearest him reached clumsily for his and spilled three or four drops.

"Oopsh...waste of good liquor. Sorry."

"Don't shed tears," Hendrin said. "There's more where that came from,"

"Sure thing. Well, here's to us all—Darrien too, damn his ugly skin!"

They drank. Then they drank some more. Hendrin matched them drink for drink, and paid for most—but his hard-shelled body quickly converted the alcohol to energy, while the Venusians grew less and less sure of their speech and coordination.

Plans took shape in the Mercurian's mind. He was here on a dangerous mission, and he knew the moment he ceased to think fast would be the moment he ceased to think.

Krodrang, Overlord of Mercury, had sent him here— Krodrang who had been content to rule the tiny planet for decades without territorial ambitions, but who suddenly had been consumed by the ambition to rule the universe as well. He had summoned Hendrin, his best agent, to the throneroom.

"I want you to go to Mars. Join Darrien's army. Get close to Darrien. And when you get the chance, steal his secrets. The Clanton Mine, the orthysynthetic duplicate robots, anything else. Bribe his henchmen. Steal his mistress. Do whatever you can—but I want Darrien's secrets! And when you have them—kill him!"

"Yes, Majesty."

In Hendrin's personal opinion the Overlord had been taken with the madness of extreme age. But it was not Hendrin's place to question. He was loyal. He accepted the job without question.

Now he was here. And he had to get to Darrien.

Pointing at the girl, he said, "What do you plan to do with her? She looks weak for a slave."

"Weak? Nonsense. She's as strong as an Earthman. They come that way, out in those colonies. We plan to bring her to Dorvis Graal, Darrien's Viceroy. Dorvis Graal will buy her and make her a slave to Darrien—or possibly a mistress."

Hendrin's black eyes narrowed. "How much will Dorvis Graal pay?"

"A hundred credas platinum, if we're lucky."

The Mercurian surveyed the girl. She was undeniably lovely, and there was something else—a smoking defiance, perhaps—that might make her an appealing challenge for a jaded tyrant. "Will you take a hundred fifty from me?"

"From *you*, Mercurian?"

"A hundred eighty, then."

The girl looked up scornfully. Her breasts heaved as she said, "You alien pigs buy and sell us as if we were cattle. But just wait! Wait until—"

The Venusian reached out and slapped her. She sank back into silence. "A hundred eighty, you say?"

Hendrin nodded. "She might keep me pleasant company on the cold nights of this accursed planet."

"I doubt it," said the soberer of the two Venusians. "She looks mean. But we'd never get a hundred eighty from Dorvis Graal. You can have her. Got the cash?"

Hendrin dropped four coins into the Venusian's leathery palm.

"Done! The girl is yours!"

The Mercurian reached across the table and imprisoned the girl's wrist in one of his huge paws. He smiled coldly as defiance flared on her face. The girl had spirit. Darrien might be interested.

CHAPTER THREE

Lon Archman shivered as the bitter Martian winds swept around him. It was just as it had been in the drug-induced tests Wentworth had run back in the Universal Intelligence office, with one little difference:

This was no dream. This was the real thing.

All he could see of Mars was the wide, flat, far-ranging plain of red sand, broken here and there by a rock outcrop or twisted gabron-weed. In the distance he could see Canalopolis, the city Darrien had taken over as the headquarters for his empire.

Archman started to walk.

After about fifteen minutes he saw his first sign of life—a guard, in the gray-and-red uniform of Darrien's men, pacing back and forth in the sand outside Canalopolis. An Earthman. He wore the leather harness that marked the renegade.

Cautiously, Archman edged forward.

Remembering what had happened in the final test on Earth, Archman glanced in all directions. Then he sprang forward, running full tilt at the unseeing renegade.

The man staggered as Archman crashed into him. Lon snatched the renegade's zam-gun and tossed it to one side. Then he grabbed the man by the scruff of his tunic and yanked him down.

He was a scrawny, hard-eyed thug with fleshless cheeks and thin lips. Archman hit him. The man crumpled like a wet paper doll.

Archman froze—listening. No one was near. He stripped off the guard's clothing, then peeled out of his own. The chill Martian winds whipped against his nakedness as he donned the guard's uniform.

Drawing his zam-gun, he incinerated his own clothing. The wind carried the particles away, and there was no trace. Then he glanced at the naked, unconscious renegade, already turning blue from cold. Without remorse Archman killed him, lifted the headless body, carried it fifty feet to a sand dune, and shoved it out of sight. Within minutes the body would be buried by tons of sand.

So far, so good. Archman tightened the uniform at the waist until it was a convincing fit. Then he plodded over the shifting sand toward the city ahead and ten minutes later he was inside Canalopolis. The guards at the gate passed him without question.

The city was old—old and filthy, like all of Mars. Streets thick with shops and bars and dark alleys, lurking strangers ready to rob or gamble or sell women; a fitting place for Darrien to have set up his empire. Dirty and dark, justice-hating like Darrien himself...

The streets were thronged with aliens of all sorts: bushy-tailed Venusians swaggering boldly with deadly stingers at the ends of their black tails; blue Mercurians, almost impregnable inside their thick shells; occasionally a Plutonian, looking like a fish with finned hands; and of course the vicious, powerful Martians showing their sneering tusks.

Here and there was an Earthman—like Darrien himself, a renegade. Archman hated these worst of all. They were betraying their home world.

He stood still and looked around. Far ahead of him, in the middle of the city, rose a vaulting palace sculptured from shimmering Martian quartz. Darrien's headquarters. Surrounding it were smaller buildings, barracks-like—and then the rest of the city sprawling in four directions.

A sign in three languages beckoned to Archman: *BAR*. He cut his way through the milling traffic and entered a long, low-ceilinged room that stank of myriad aliens. A Martian bartender stood before a formidable array of exotic bottles; along the bar, men of five worlds slumped in varying degrees of drunkenness. Further back, lit by a couple of dusty, sputtering levon-tubes, there were some secluded booths.

Archman stiffened suddenly. In one of the booths was a sight that brought quick anger. A blue Mercurian was leaning over, lasciviously pawing a near-nude, sobbing Earthgirl. There were two Venusians in the booth with them, both lying face-down in pools of slop.

Archman shouldered past a couple of drozky-winos at the bar, choking back his disgust, and moved toward the booth in the back...

"Hello, Mercurian. Nice piece of flesh you've got there."

"Isn't she, though? I just bought her from these slobs." The Mercurian indicated the drunken Venusians, and laughed. "We ought to cut their tails off before they wake up."

Archman eyed the alien stonily. "They wear Darrien's uniform. That's more than you can say, stranger."

"Don't leap to conclusions. I'm as loyal to Darrien as you are, maybe more so. I'm here to join up."

"Sorry. Mind if I sit down?"

"Dump one of the tailed ones on the floor."

Casually Archman shoved one of the Venusians. The alien stirred, moaned, and slid to the floor. Archman took his seat, feeling the girl's warmness next to him.

"My name's Archman," he said. "Yours?"

"Hendrin. Just arrived from Mercury. A fine wench, isn't she?"

Archman studied the girl. Her face was set in sullen defiance, and despite her near-nudity she had a firm dignity about her. She seemed to be staring right through the Mercurian rather than at him, and the fact that her breasts were nearly bare and her lovely legs unclad hardly disturbed her.

"Where are you from, lass?"

"Is it your business—*traitor?*"

"Harsh words. But perhaps we've met somewhere on Earth. I'm curious."

"I'm not from Earth. I was a colonist on Planetoid Eleven until—until—"

"An attractive bit of property." Archman smiled casually. "I could use her myself. Would you take a hundred credas?"

"I paid a hundred eighty."

"Two hundred, then?"

"Not for a thousand," said the Mercurian firmly. "This girl is for Darrien himself."

"Beasts," the girl muttered.

The Mercurian slapped her with a clawed fist. A little trickle of blood seeped from the corner of her mouth.

Archman forced himself to watch coldly. "You won't sell, eh?"

"I sure won't," said the Mercurian exultantly. "Darrien will go wild when he sees this one!"

"What if he takes her away from you?"

"Darrien wouldn't do that. He knows how to keep the loyalty of his men." The Mercurian rose, clutching the girl's wrist. "Come, lovely. And as for you, Earthman, it was good to make your acquaintance. Perhaps we'll meet again someday."

"Perhaps," Archman said tightly. He sat back and watched as the Mercurian, gloating, led his prize away. A flash of thighs, the bright warmness of a breast; then girl and captor were gone.

This is a filthy business, Archman thought bitterly. He threw a coin on the table and followed the pair into the street.

Hendrin the Mercurian moved through the streets of Canalopolis, dragging the sobbing girl after him.

"You don't have to pull me," she moaned, struggling with her free hand to pull together the tatters of her clothing. "I don't want my arm yanked out. I'll come willingly."

"Then walk faster," Hendrin grunted. He peered ahead, toward the rosy bulk of Darrien's palace as a plan formed in his mind. Using the girl as a pawn, he could gain access to the palace.

But in all probability he'd see, not the real Darrien, but an orthysynthetic duplicate of the shrewd leader. One false move and Hendrin would find himself brain-burned and tossed out as carrion for the sandwolves. This had to be done carefully, very carefully.

"Why do you have to do this to me?" the girl asked suddenly. "Why couldn't I have been left on Planetoid Eleven with my parents, in peace, instead of being dragged here, to be paraded nude through the streets of this awful city and—" She gasped for breath.

"Easy, girl, easy. That's a great many words for your soft throat to spew out so quickly."

"Why am I being sold to Darrien? What will he do to me?"

"I'm selling you for money—"

"But those Venusians said you bid more for me than Darrien would have paid."

"They were drunk. They didn't recognize a prize specimen when they saw one."

"*Prize specimen!*" She spat the words back at him. "To you aliens I'm just a prize specimen, is that it?"

"I'm afraid so," Hendrin said lightly. "As for what Darrien will do to you—that ought to be obvious!"

"But why does life have to be this way? That Earthman, back in the bar—doesn't he have any loyalty to someone of his own world?"

"Apparently not. Enough of this talk; what's your name?"

"Elissa Hall."

"A pretty name, though a trifle too smooth for my taste. How old are you?"

"Nineteen."

"Umm. Darrien will be interested."

"You're the most cold-blooded creature I've ever met," she said.

Hendrin chuckled dryly. "I doubt it. I'm a kindly old saint compared with Darrien. I'm just doing my job, lady; don't make it hard for me."

She didn't answer. Hendrin rotated one eye until he had a good view of her. She had blonde hair cut in bangs, blue eyes, a pert nose, warm-looking lips. Her figure was excellent. During a less important time, Hendrin might have had some sport with her first. But not now. Like all his people, the Mercurian was cold and businesslike when it came to a job. And much as he would have liked the idea, it didn't fit into the strategy.

"Halt and state name," snapped a guard suddenly, presenting a zam-gun. He was a Martian, grinning ferociously.

"Hendrin's my name. I'm a member of Darrien's raiders, and I'm bringing this girl to sell to him."

The Martian studied Elissa brazenly, then said, "Very well. You can pass. Take her to Dorvis Graal's office. He'll talk to you."

Hendrin moved past the guard and into the compound of buildings surrounding Darrien's lofty palace.

Dorvis Graal, Darrien's Viceroy and the Chief of Canalopolis' Security Police, was a Venusian. He looked up from a cluttered desk as Hendrin and the girl entered.

There was a bleak, crafty glint in his faceted eyes; his beak of a nose seemed to jab forward at the Mercurian, and the deadly stinging-tail flicked ominously.

"Who are you, Mercurian?"

"The name is Hendrin. I've recently joined Darrien's forces."

"Odd. I don't remember seeing a record on you."

Hendrin shrugged. "All I know is I signed on to fight for Darrien, and I have something I think might interest him."

"You mean the girl?" Dorvis Graal said. He squinted at her. "She's an Earth colonist, isn't she?"

"From Planetoid Eleven. I think our lord Darrien might like her."

Dorvis Graal chuckled harshly. "Possibly he will— but if he does there'll be the devil to pay when Meryola, Darrien's mistress, finds out!"

"That's Darrien's problem," the blue Mercurian said. "But I'm in need of cash. How can I see Darrien?"

"Darrien wouldn't bother with you. What would you consider a fair price for the wench?"

"Two hundred credas and a captaincy in Darrien's forces."

The Venusian smiled derisively. "Mars has two moons. Why not ask for one of those?"

"I've named my price," said Hendrin.

"Let me look at the girl." Dorvis Graal rose, flicking his bushy tail from side to side. "These rags obscure the view," he said, ripping away what remained of Elissa's clothing. Her body, thus revealed, was pure white for a moment—until suffused by a bright pink blush. She tried to cover herself with her hands, but Dorvis Graal slapped them away.

After a lengthy appraisal he looked up. "A fair wench. Perhaps Darrien will expend a hundred credas or so. Certainly no more."

"And the captaincy?"

"I can always ask," said the Venusian mockingly.

Hendrin frowned. "What do you mean, *you* can ask? Can't I talk to Darrien?"

"I'll handle the transaction. Darrien doesn't care to be bothered by every Mercurian who wanders in with a bare bottomed beauty he's picked up in a raid. You wait here. I'll show him the girl."

"Sorry," Hendrin said quickly. He threw his cloak over the girl's shoulders. "Either I see Darrien myself or it's no deal. I'll keep the girl myself rather than let you cheat me out of her."

Dorvis Graal's whip-like tail went rigid for an instant—but then, as he saw Hendrin apparently meant what he said, he relaxed. "I'll let you in," he said. "I'll let you see Darrien and take him the girl. It's rare to let a common soldier in, but in this case perhaps it can be done."

"And how much do I bribe you?"

"Crudely put," said the Venusian. "I ask no money. Just that if Darrien, doesn't want her, I get her. Free."

Hendrin scowled, but he'd expected that. It was too bad for the girl, of course, but what of that? At least he'd definitely get to see Darrien this way—which was his whole plan. And the chance of Darrien's turning down the girl was slim. "How do I reach Darrien?"

"I'll give you a pass to the tunnel leading to the throneroom. The rest is up to you. But remember this: you won't live long if you try to cheat me."

"I'm a man of my word," Hendrin said, meaning it. He accepted the pass from Dorvis Graal, grinned wolfishly, and seized the girl's arm. "Which way do I go?"

"The tunnel entrance is down there," Dorvis Graal said, pointing. "And here's hoping Darrien isn't in a buying mood today," He leered suggestively as Hendrin led the girl away. Either way the girl could hardly win.

CHAPTER FOUR

Lon Archman had watched the Mercurian and the girl disappear into Dorvis Graal's office. He had followed them this far without difficulty but the opportunity for action seemed to have passed him by. It was too late to overpower the Mercurian and take the girl from the Planetoids to Darrien himself.

Or was it?

The door of Dorvis Graal's office opened and Hendrin and the girl stepped out into the street again. Archman saw that the girl no longer wore her tattered clothes; she had evidently been stripped bare in the Viceroy's office. Now she wore the Mercurian's cloak loosely around her shoulders, but it concealed little.

And Hendrin was clutching some sort of paper in his hand. A pass? It had to be. A pass to see Darrien!

Archman broke from the shadows and ran toward Dorvis Graal's office just as girl and Mercurian disappeared through another doorway.

But a figure loomed to intercept him before he traveled more than a dozen paces. A stiff-armed fist hurled him back, and he stared into the barrel of a cocked zam-gun.

"Where are you heading so fast?" The speaker was a Martian guard.

"I have to see Dorvis Graal. It's on a matter of high treason! Darrien's in danger of an assassin!"

The Martian's expression shifted from one of hostility to keen interest. "Are you lying?"

"Of course not, you fool. Get out of my way and let me get to the Viceroy before it's too late!"

The zam-gun was holstered and Archman burst past. He reached Dorvis Graal's office, flung open the door, and bowed humbly to the glittering-eyed Venusian who looked up in some astonishment.

"Who are you? What's the meaning of this?"

"I'm Lon Archman of Darrien's brigade. Quick! Have a Mercurian and a girl been through here in the last minute or so?"

"Yes. What business is it of yours?"

"That Mercurian's an assassin!" Archman got as much excitement into his voice as he could manage. "I've been following him all morning. He intends to kill Darrien!"

A mixture of emotions played suddenly over the Viceroy's face—greed, fear, curiosity, disbelief. "Indeed? Well, that can easily be stopped. He's in the tunnel, on the way to Darrien. I'll have the tunnel guards intercept him and send him up to Froljak the Interrogator. Thanks for your information."

"I'd like to go after him myself."

"What?"

"I want to kill that Mercurian! I don't want your tunnel guards to do it."

"They're not going to kill him," Dorvis Graal said impatiently. "They'll hold him for questioning. If you're telling the truth that he's an assassin—"

Archman scowled. This wasn't getting him into the tunnel, where he wanted to go. "Let me go after him, sir," he pleaded. "As a reward. A reward for telling you. I want to be in on the capture."

Dorvis Graal seemed to relent. It was pretty flimsy, Archman thought, but maybe—

"All right. Here's a pass, the Viceroy said, "Get going, now—and report back to me when it's all over."

Archman seized the pass and streaked for the tunnel.

After he had left, Dorvis Graal lifted the speaking-tube. "Holgo?"

"Yes, sir?"

"Has a Mercurian passed through the tunnels yet? He's got a naked wench with him."

"Yes, sir. He and the girl came by this way two minutes ago. He had a pass, so I let him through. Is there anything wrong?"

"No—no, not at all," Dorvis Graal said. If the Mercurian reached Darrien safely, which he seemed likely to do, he'd probably not be facing the leader himself but only an expendable orthysynthetic duplicate. There was always time to catch him, if he really were the assassin.

And as for the Earthman—well, just to be safe Dorvis Graal decided to pick him up. He had seemed a little too eager to get into the tunnel.

Dorvis Graal spoke again into the tube, "There's an Earthman coming into the tunnel now. He's got a pass, but I want you to pick him up and hold him for questioning."

"Yes, sir."

Dorvis Graal broke the contact and sat back. He wondered which one was lying, the Mercurian or the

Earthman—or both. And just what would happen if an assassin reached Darrien.

Perhaps, Dorvis Graal thought, it might mean I'd reach power. Perhaps.

He smiled and contemplated the possibilities.

Hendrin reached the end of the long corridor and folded Dorvis Graal's pass in his pocket. He would probably need it to get out again.

He turned to the girl. "Pull the cloak tight around you. I don't want Darrien to see your nakedness until the proper moment. And try to brighten up and look more desirable."

"Why should I care what I look like?"

Patiently the Mercurian said, "Because if Darrien doesn't buy you I have to give you to that Venusian out there. And, believe me, you'll be a lot better off with Darrien than in the arms of that foul-smelling tailed one. So cheer up; it's the lesser of the two evils." He closed the cloak around her and together they advanced toward Darrien's throneroom.

A stony-faced Martian guard stood outside the throneroom. "What would you with Darrien?"

"I bring him a girl." Hendrin pointed to Elissa, then showed the guard Dorvis Graal's pass. "The Viceroy himself sent me to Darrien."

The Martian grunted. He opened the door and Hendrin stepped in.

It was a scene of utter magnificence. The vast room was lined from wall to wall with a fantastically costly yangskin rug, except in the very center, where a depression had been scooped out and a small pool created. In the pool two nude Earthgirls swam, writhing sinuously for Darrien's delight.

Darrien. Hendrin's eyes slowly turned toward the throne at the side of the vast room. It was a bright platinum pedestal upon which Darrien and his mistress sat. Hendrin studied them while waiting to be noticed.

So that's Darrien—or his double. The galaxy's most brilliant and most evil man sat tensely on his throne, beady eyes darting here and there, radiating an unmistakably malevolent intelligence. Darrien was a small, shrunken man, his face a complex network of wrinkles and valleys. Darrien or his double, Hendrin reminded himself again. The possibility was slim that Darrien himself was here; more likely he was elsewhere in the palace, operating the dummy on the throne by a remote-control device he himself had conceived.

And at Darrien's side, the lovely Meryola, Darrien's mistress. She was clad in filmy vizosheen that revealed more than it hid, and the Mercurian was startled at the beauty revealed. It was known that Meryola's beauty was enhanced by drugs from Darrien's secret laboratories, but even so she was ravishing in her own right.

Hendrin had to admire Darrien. After the destruction of Venusia five years ago, a lesser man might have drifted into despair—but not Darrien. Goaded by the fierce rage and desire for vengeance he had simply moved on to Mars and established here a kingdom twice as magnificent as that the Earthmen had destroyed on Venus.

He was talking now to a pair of bushy-tailed Venusians who stood before the throne. Lieutenants, obviously, receiving some sort of instructions. Finally

Darrien was through. The tyrant looked up and fixed Hendrin in his piercing gaze.

"Who are you, Mercurian, and what do you want here?"

Darrien's voice was astonishingly deep and forceful. For a moment Hendrin was shaken by the man's commanding tones.

Then he said, "I be Hendrin, sire, of your majesty's legions. I bring with me a girl whom perhaps—"

"I might purchase," snapped Darrien. "That fool Dorvis Graal! He knows well that I can't be troubled with such petty things."

"Begging your pardon, sire," Hendrin said with glib humility, "but the Viceroy said that this girl was of such surpassing beauty that he couldn't set a proper price himself, and sent me to you with her."

Hendrin saw an interesting series of reactions taking place on the face of the tyrant's mistress. Meryola had been staring curiously at the girl, who stood slumped beneath the shapeless cloak. As Hendrin spoke, Meryola seemed to stiffen as if fearing a rival; her breasts, half-visible through her gauzy garment, rose and fell faster, and her eyes flashed. Hendrin smiled inwardly. There were possibilities here.

Darrien was frowning, bringing even more wrinkles to his face. Finally he said, "Well, then, let's see this paragon of yours. Unveil her. But if she's not all you say, both of you shall die, and Dorvis Graal in the bargain!"

Hendrin approached the girl. "Three lives depend on your beauty, now—including your own."

"Why should I want to live?" she murmured.

Hendrin ignored it and ripped away the cloak. Elissa stood before Darrien totally nude. She stood tall and proud, her breasts outthrust, her pale body quivering as if with desire. Darrien stared at her for a long moment. Meryola, by his side, seemed ready to explode.

At length Darrien said, "You may live. She is a lovely creature. Cover her again."

Hendrin obediently tossed the cloak over her shoulders and bowed to Darrien.

"Name your price."

"Two hundred credas—and a captaincy in your forces."

He held his breath. Darrien turned to Elissa.

"How old are you, girl?"

"Nineteen."

"Has this Mercurian laid lustful hands on you?"

"I've never been with any man, sire," the girl said, blushing.

"Umm." To Hendrin Darrien said, "The captaincy is yours, and *five* hundred credas. Come, girl; let me show you where your quarters will be."

Darrien rose from the throne, and Hendrin was surprised to see the man was a dwarf, no more than four feet high. He strode rapidly down the pedestal to Elissa's side. She was more than a foot taller than he.

He led her away. Hendrin, his head bowed, glanced up slowly and saw Meryola fuming on the throne. Now was the time to act, he thought. Now.

"Your highness!" he whispered.

She looked down at him. "I should have you flayed," she said harshly. "Do you know what you've done?"

"I fear I've brought your Highness a rival," Hendrin said. "For this I beg your pardon; I had no way of knowing Darrien sought concubines for himself. And I sorely needed the money."

"Enough," Meryola said. Her face was black with anger, but still radiant. "Out of my sight, and let me deal with the problem you've brought me."

"A moment, milady. May I speak?"

"Speak," she said impatiently.

He stared at her smoldering gray-flecked eyes. "Milady, I wish to undo the damage I've caused you this day."

"How could you do that?"

Hendrin thought quickly. "If you'll go to my lord Darrien and occupy his attention for the next hour, I'll slip within and find the girl. You need only sign an order testifying that she's a traitor to Darrien, and I'll convey her to the dungeons—where she'll die before Darrien knows she's missing."

Meryola glanced at him curiously. "You're a strange one. First you bring this ravishing creature to Darrien—then, when his back is turned, you offer to remove her again. Odd loyalty, Mercurian!"

Hendrin saw that he had blundered. "I but meant, milady, that I had no idea my act would have such consequences. I want the chance to redeem myself—for to bring a shadow between Darrien and Meryola would be to weaken all of our hopes."

"Nicely spoken," Meryola said, and Hendrin realized he had recovered control. He looked at her bluntly now, saw tiny crows' feet beginning to show at the edges of her eyes. She was a lovely creature, but an aging one. He knew that she would be ultimately of great use to him.

"Very well," she said. "I'll endeavor to separate Darrien from his new plaything—and while I'm amusing our lord get you inside and take the girl away, I'll double his five hundred credas if he never sees her again."

"I thank you," Hendrin said. The Mercurian offered her his arm as she dismounted from the throne. He felt a current of anticipation tingling in him. He was on his way, now. Already he had won Darrien's approval—and, if he could only manage to convey the girl to the dungeons without Darrien's discovering who had done it, he would be in the favor of the tyrant's mistress as well.

Legend had it that only Meryola knew when Darrien himself, sat on the throne and when a duplicate. He would need her help.

Quietly he slipped from the throne room in search of Elissa.

CHAPTER FIVE

The entrance to the tunnel was guarded by two Venusians and a fin-handed Plutonian. Lon Archman approached and said, "Is this the way to Darrien's throneroom?"

"It is. What would you want there?"

Archman flashed the Viceroy's pass. "This is all the explanation you should need."

They stepped aside and allowed him through. The corridor was long and winding and lit by the bright glow of levon-tubes. There was no sign of the Mercurian or the girl up ahead.

That was all right, Archman thought. He had no particular interest in them. His ruse had worked. Here he was, with a pass to the throneroom.

He rounded a bend in the corridor and halted suddenly. Three Martians blocked his way, forming a solid bar across the tunnel.

"Stay right there, Earthman."

"I've got a pass from Dorvis Graal," he snapped impatiently. "Let me go." He smelled the foul musk of the Martians as they clustered around him.

"Hand over the pass."

Suspiciously Archman gave up the slip. The Martian read it, nodded complacently, and ripped the pass into a dozen pieces, which he scattered in the air.

"You can't do that! Dorvis Graal—"

"Dorvis Graal himself has just phoned me to revoke your pass," the Martian informed him. "You're to be held for questioning as a possible assassin."

Grimly Archman saw what had happened. His 97.003% rating had fooled him into thinking he was some sort of superman. Naturally, the Viceroy had been suspicious of the strange-faced, overeager Earthman with the wild story, and had ordered his pickup. Possibly the Mercurian and the girl were safely inside. Or else they had been picked up too. It didn't make any difference. The wily Viceroy was taking no chances.

Archman's zam-gun was in his hand, and a second later the Martian's tusked face was a blossoming nightmare, the features disappearing in a crackle of atomized dust. The man sagged to the floor. Archman turned on the other two, but they had moved into action. A club descended with stunning force on his arm and the zam-gun dropped from his fist. He struck out feeling a stiff jolt of pain run through him as he connected.

"Dorvis Graal said not to kill him," one of the Martians cautioned.

Archman whirled, trying to keep eyes on both of them at once. It was impossible. As one rocked back from the force of the Earthman's blow, the other drew near. Archman felt hot breath behind him, turned—

A copperwood club crashed against the side of his head. He fought desperately for consciousness. The club hit him again and a searing tide of pain swept up around him, blotting out tunnel and Martians and everything.

Hendrin confronted the shivering Elissa. She stood before a mirror clad only in a single sheer garment Darrien had given her.

"Come with me," he whispered. "Now, before Darrien comes back."

"Where will you take me?"

"Away from here. I'll hide you in the dungeons until it's safe to get you out. Now that I've been paid, I don't feel any need to give you to Darrien—and the tyrant's mistress will pay me double to get you out."

"I suppose I'll then be subject to your tender mercies again—until the next time you decide to sell me. Sorry, but I'm not going. I'll take my chances here. Darrien probably takes good care of his women."

"Meryola will kill you!"

"Possibly. But how long could I live with you outside? No, I'll stay here, now that you've sold me."

Hendrin cursed and pulled her to him. He hit her once, carefully, on the chin. She shuddered and went sprawling backward; he caught her—she was surprisingly light—and tossed her over his shoulder. Footsteps were audible at the door.

He glanced around, found a rear exit, slipped through, and saw a staircase. The Mercurian, bearing his unconscious burden, ran. Darrien's men followed them.

Through a dim haze of pain Lon Archman heard voices. Someone was speaking in a Martian's guttural tones. "Put this one in a cell, will you?"

Another voice, with a Plutonian's liquid accents, "Strange the dungeons should be so busy at this hour. A few moments ago a Mercurian brought an Earthgirl here to be kept safe—a would-be assassin, I'm told."

"As is this one. Here, lock him up. Dorvis Graal will be here to interrogate him later."

"That means two executions tomorrow," said the Plutonian gleefully.

"Two?"

"Yes. The Lady Meryola sent me instructions just before you came that the Earthgirl is to die in the morning. The jailer chuckled. "I think I'll put 'em in the same cell."

Archman felt himself being thrown roughly into a cold room, heard a door clang shut behind him. He opened one eye painfully. Someone was sobbing elsewhere in the cell.

He looked. It was the Earthgirl, the one the Mercurian had been with. She lay in a crumpled, pathetic little heap in the far corner of the cell. After a moment she looked up.

"It's you—the Earthman!"

He nodded.

A spasm of sobbing shook her.

"Ease up," Archman said. He winced at the pain that flashed up and down his own battered body. "Stop crying!"

"Stop crying! Why? They are going to kill us both tomorrow!"

In the darkness of the cell, Archman eyed the shadow-etched figure of the girl uneasily. He was twenty-three; he had spent six years in Universal Intelligence, including his training period. That made him capable of handling tusked Martians and finny

Plutonians with ease, but a sobbing Earthgirl—? There were no rules in the book for that.

Suddenly the girl sat up, and Archman saw her wipe her eyes. "Why am I crying?" she asked. "I should be happy. Tomorrow they're going to kill me—and that's the greatest favor I could wish for."

"Don't talk like that!"

"Why not? Ever since Darrien's raiders grabbed me on Planetoid Eleven, I've just been bought and sold over and over, bargained for, used as a pawn in one maneuver after another. Do you think I care if they kill me now?"

Archman was silent. Flickering rays of light from somewhere outside bobbed at random in the cell, illuminating the girl's almost bare form from time to time. He wanted to talk gently to her, to take her in his arms, to comfort her—

But he couldn't. He was a trained assassin, not a smooth-talking romancer. The words wouldn't come, and he crouched back on his heels, feeling the throbbing pain from his beating heart and the even sharper pain of not being able to speak.

It was the girl who broke the silence. She said, "And what of you? You're a renegade, a traitor to your home world. How will you feel when you die tomorrow? Clean?"

"You don't understand," Archman said tightly. "I'm not—" He paused. He didn't dare to reveal the true nature of his mission.

Or did he? What difference did it make? In an hour or so, he would be taken to the Interrogator—and most assuredly they would pry from his unwilling subconscious the truth. Why not tell the girl now and at least go to death without *her* hating him? The conflict within him was brief and searing.

"You're not what?" she asked sarcastically.

"I'm not a renegade," he said, his voice leaden. "You don't understand me. You don't know me."

"I know that you're a coldblooded calculating murderer. Do I need to know anything else, Archman?"

He drew close to her and stared evenly at her. In a harsh whisper he said, "I'm an Intelligence agent. I'm here to assassinate Darrien."

There, he thought. He'd made his confession to her. It didn't matter if the cell were tapped, though he doubted it—the Interrogator would dredge the information from him soon enough.

She met his gaze. "Oh," she said simply.

"That changes things, doesn't it? I mean—you don't hate me any more, do you?"

She laughed—a cold tinkle of a sound. "Hate you? Do you expect me to *love* you, simply because you're on the same side I am? You're still cold-blooded. You're still a killer. And I hate killers!"

"But—" He let his voice die away, realizing it was hopeless. The girl was embittered; he'd never convince her that he was anything but a killing machine, and it didn't matter which side he was on. He rose and walked to the far corner of the cell. He remained silent.

After a few moments he said, "I don't even know your name."

"Do you care?"

"You're my cellmate on the last night of my life. I'd like to know."

"Elissa, Elissa Hall."

He wanted to say, *it's a pretty name,* but his tongue was tied by shame and anger. Bitterly he stared at the blank wall of the cell, reflecting that this was an ironic situation. Here he was, locked in a cell with a practically nude girl, and—

He stiffened. "Do you hear something?"

"No."

"I do. Listen."

"Yes," she said a moment later. "I hear it!"

Footsteps. The footsteps of the Interrogator.

CHAPTER SIX

Cautiously, the blue Mercurian touched the stud of the door-communicator just outside Meryola's suite.

"Who's there?" The voice was languid, vibrant.

"Hendrin. The Mercurian."

"Come in, won't you?"

The door slid aside and Hendrin entered. Meryola's chamber was as luxuriously appointed a suite as he had ever seen. Clinging damasks, woven with elaborate designs and figures, draped themselves artistically over the windows; a subtle fragrance lingered in the air, and, from above, warm jampulla-rays glowed, heating and sterilizing the air, preserving Meryola's beauty.

As for Meryola herself, she lay nude on a plush yangskin rug, bronzing herself beneath a raylamp. As Hendrin entered, she rose coyly, stretched, and without sign of embarrassment casually donned a filmy robe. She approached Hendrin, and the usually unemotional Mercurian found himself strangely moved by her beauty.

"Well?" Her tone was business-like now.

"You ask of the girl?"

"Of what else?"

Hendrin smiled. "The girl has been disposed of. She lies in the dungeon below."

"Has anyone seen you take her there? The mistress of the wardrobe, perhaps? That one's loyal to Darrien, and hates me; I suspect she was once Darrien's woman, before she aged." A shadow of anger passed over Meryola's lovely face, as if she were contemplating a fate in store for herself.

"No one saw me, your highness. I induced her to leave the wardrobe-room and took her there by the back stairs. I handed her over to the jailer with orders to keep her imprisoned indefinitely. I gave him a hundred credas."

Meryola nodded approvingly. She crossed the room, moving with the grace of a Mercurian sun-tiger, and snatched a speaking-tube from the wall.

"Dungeons," she ordered.

A moment later Hendrin heard a voice respond, and Meryola said, "Was an Earthgirl brought to you just now by a large Mercurian? Good. The girl is to die at once; these are my orders. No, fool, no written confirmation is needed. The girl's a traitor to Darrien; what more do you need but my word? Very well."

She broke the contact and turned back to. Hendrin. "She dies at once, Mercurian. You've been faithful. Faithful, and shrewd—for Darrien pays you to bring the girl here, and Meryola pays you to take her away."

She opened a drawer, took out a small leather pouch, handed it to Hendrin. Tactfully he accepted it without opening it and slipped it into his sash.

"Your servant, milady."

Inwardly he felt mildly regretful; the girl *had* come in for raw treatment. But soon she'd be out of her misery. In a way, it was unfortunate; with the girl alive he might have had further power over Meryola. Still, he had gained access to the palace, which was a basic objective, and he had won the gratitude of Darrien's mistress, which was the second step. As for the third—

"Lord Darrien will be angry when he finds the girl is missing, milady. There's no chance he'll accuse me—"

"Of course not. He'll be angry for a moment or two, but I think *I'll* be able to console him." She yawned delicately, and for an instant her gown fluttered open. She did not hurry to close it. Hendrin wondered if, perhaps, she longed for some variety after five years of Darrien's embraces.

"Our master must be pleased to have one so fair as you," the blue Mercurian said. He moved a little closer to Meryola, and she did not seem to object. "Legend has it that he trusts you with his inmost secrets—such as the identity of his robot duplicates."

Meryola chuckled archly. "So the galaxy knows of the orthysynthetics, eh? Darrien's Achilles heel, so to speak. I thought it was a secret."

"It is as widely known as your loveliness," Hendrin said. He was nearly touching Meryola by now—

Frowning curiously, she reached out and touched his bare shoulder. She rubbed her forefinger over the Mercurian's hard shell and commented, "You blue ones are far from thin-skinned, I see."

"Our planet's climate is a rigorous one, milady. The shell is needed."

"So I would imagine. Rough-feeling stuff, isn't it? I wonder what the feel of it against my whole body would be like…"

Smiling, Hendrin said, "If milady would know—"

She edged closer to him. He felt a quiver of triumph; through Meryola, he could learn the secret of Darrien's robot duplicates. He extended his massive arms and gently caressed her shoulders.

She seemed to melt into him. The Mercurian started to fold her in his arms. Then his hypersensitive ears picked up the sound of relays clicking in the door.

In one quick motion he had pushed her away and bent stiffly, kneeling in an attitude of utter devotion. It was none too soon. Before she had a chance to register surprise, the door opened.

Darrien entered.

Lon Archman crouched in the far corner of the cell, listening to the talk going on outside.

A cold Martian voice was saying, "There's an Earthman here. Dorvis Graal wants him brought to Froljak the Interrogator for some questions."

"Certainly." It was the Plutonian jailer who spoke. "And how about the girl? Do you want her too?"

"Girl? What girl? My orders say only to get the Earthman. I don't know anything about a girl."

"Very well. I'll give you the man only." The Plutonian giggled thickly. "And when Froljak's through with him, I guess you can bring the shattered shell back to me and I'll put it out of its misery. Froljak is very thorough."

"Yes," the Martian said ominously. "Take me to the cell."

Suddenly Archman was conscious of the girl's warmth against him, of her breasts and thighs clinging to him.

"They're going to take you away!" she said. "They're going to leave me here alone."

"A moment ago you said you hated me," Archman reminded her bluntly.

She ignored him. "I don't want to die," she sobbed. "Don't let them kill me."

"You'll be on your own now. I'm going to be Interrogated." He shuddered slightly. The capital "I" on "Interrogated" was all too meaningful. It was an inquisition he would never survive.

"Is this the cell?" the Martian asked, outside.

"That's right. They're both in there."

The cell-door began to open. Elissa huddled sobbing on the floor. Archman realized he had been a fool to give up so easily, to even allow the thought of death to enter his mind while he still lived.

"When the Martian comes in," he whispered, "throw yourself at his feet. Beg for mercy; do anything. Just distract him."

Her sobbing stopped, and she nodded.

Archman flattened himself against the wall. The Martian, a burly, broad-shouldered, heavy-tusked specimen, entered the cell.

"Come, Earthman. Time for some questions."

Elissa rose and leaped forward. She threw herself at the Martian, groveling before him, clasping his ankles appealingly.

"What? Who are you?"

"Don't let them kill me! Please—I don't want to die! I'll do anything! Just get me out of here!"

The Martian frowned.

"This must be the Earthgirl," he muttered. To Elissa he said, "I'm not here for you. I want the Earthman. Is he here?"

"Don't let them kill me!" Elissa wailed again, wrapping herself around the Martian's legs.

Archman sprang.

He hit the Martian squarely amidships, and the evil-smelling breath left the alien in one grunted gust. At the same moment Elissa's supplication turned into an attack; with all her strength she tugged at the surprised Martian, knocked him off balance.

The zam-gun flared and ashed a chunk of the wall. Archman drove a fist into the Martian's corded belly, and the alien staggered. Archman hit him again, and smashed upward from the floor to shatter a tusk. A gout of Martian blood spurted.

The Martian thrashed about wildly; Archman saw a blow catch Elissa and hurl her heavily against the wall. He redoubled his own efforts and within moments had efficiently reduced the Martian to a sagging mass of semi-conscious flesh, nothing more. He seized the zam-gun.

"Elissa! Come on!"

But the girl was slumped unconscious on the floor. He took a hesitant step toward her, then whirled as a voice behind him cried, "What's all the noise around here?"

It was the Plutonian jailer. And the door was beginning to close.

Nimbly Archman leaped through, as the micronite door clanged shut on the girl and the unconscious Martian. The Plutonian had done whatever had to be done to close the cell door. Now he was fumbling for a weapon.

The fish-man's wide mouth bobbed in astonishment as Archman sprang toward him.

"The Earthman! How—who—?"

Viciously Archman jabbed the zam-gun between the spread lips and fired. The Plutonian died without a whimper, his head incinerated instantly.

Archman turned back to the door. He heard Elissa's faint cries within.

But there was no sign of a lever. How did the door open? He ran up and down the length of the cell block, looking for some control that would release the girl.

There was none.

"Step back from the door. I'm going to try to blast it open."

He turned the zam-gun to full force and cut loose. The micronite door glowed briefly, but that was all. A mere zam-gun wouldn't break through.

Angrily Archman kicked at the door, and a hollow boom resounded. Time was running short, and the girl was irretrievably locked in. The door obviously worked on some secret principle known only to the jailers, and there was no chance for him to discover the secret now.

"Elissa—can you hear me?"

"Yes," Faintly.

"There's no way I can get you out. I can't stay here; there's certain to be someone here before long."

"Go, then. Leave me here. There's no sense in both of us being trapped."

He smiled. There seemed to be a warmth in her voice that had been absent before. "Good girl," he said. "Sorry—but—"

"That's all right. You'd better hurry!"

Archman turned, stepped over the fallen form of the Plutonian jailer, and dashed the length of the dungeon, toward the winding stairs that led upward. He had no idea where he was heading; he only knew he had to escape.

The stairs were dark; visibility was poor. He ran at top speed, zam-gun holstered but ready to fly into action at instant's notice.

He rounded a curve in the staircase and started on the next flight. Suddenly a massive figure stepped out of the shadows on the landing, and before Archman could do anything he felt himself enmeshed in a giant's grip.

CHAPTER SEVEN

Hendrin froze in the kneeling position, waiting for Darrien to enter the room.

The diminutive tyrant wore a loose saffron robe, and he was frowning grimly. Hendrin wondered if this were the real Darrien, or the duplicate he had seen before—or perhaps another duplicate entirely.

"You keep strange company, Meryola," Darrien said icily. "I thought to find you alone."

Hendrin rose and faced Darrien. "Sire—"

"Oh! The Mercurian who brought me the fair wench! I'm glad to see you here too. I have a question for the two of you."

"Which is?" Meryola asked.

Instead of answering, Darrien paced jerkily around the chamber, peering here and there. Finally he looked up.

"The girl," he boomed. "Elissa. What have you done with her?"

Hendrin stared blankly at Darrien, grateful for the hard mask of a Mercurian's face that kept him from betraying his emotions. As for Meryola, she merely sneered.

"Your new plaything, Darrien? I haven't seen her since this Mercurian unveiled her before you."

"Hmm, Hendrin, what were you doing here, anyway?"

The Mercurian tensed.

"Milady wished to speak to me," he said, throwing the ball to her. In a situation like this it didn't pay to be a gentleman. "I was about to receive her commands when you entered, sire."

"Well, Meryola?"

She favored Hendrin with a black look and said, "I was about to send the Mercurian on an errand to the perfumers' shop. My stocks are running low."

Darrien chuckled. "Clever, but you've done better, I fear. There are plenty of wenches around who'll run your errands—and your supply of perfumes was replenished but yesterday." The little man's eyes burnt brightly with the flame of his malevolent intelligence. "I don't know why you try to fool me, Meryola, but I'll be charitable and accept your word for more than it's worth."

He fixed both of them with a cold stare. "I suspect you two of a conspiracy against Elissa—and you, Mercurian, are particularly suspect. Meryola, you'll pay if the girl's been harmed. And, Hendrin—I want the girl back."

"Sire, I—"

"No discussion! Mercurian, bring back the girl before nightfall, or you'll die!"

Darrien scowled blackly at both of them, then turned sharply on his heel and stalked out. Despite his four feet of height, he seemed an awesome, commanding figure.

The door closed loudly.

"I didn't expect that," Meryola said. "But I should have. Darrien is almost impossible to deceive."

"What do we do now?" Hendrin said. "The girl, milady—"

"The girl is in the dungeons, awaiting execution. She'll be dead before Darrien discovers where she is."

Hendrin rubbed his domelike head. "You heard what Darrien said, though. Either I produce the girl or I die. Do you think he'll go through with it?"

"Darrien always means what he says. Unfortunately for you, so do I." She stared coldly at him. "The girl is in the dungeons. Leave her there. If you *do* produce the girl alive—*I'll* have you killed!"

Hendrin nodded unhappily. "Milady—"

"No more, now. Get away from me before Darrien returns. I want to take his mind off Elissa until the execution's past. Then it will be too late for him to complain. Leave me."

Baffled, Hendrin turned away and passed through the door into the hallway, which was dimly lit with levon-tubes. He leaned against the wall for a moment, brooding and thinking it over.

Events had taken a deadly turn. He had interposed himself between Darrien and Meryola, and now he was doomed either way. If he failed to restore Elissa to Darrien, the tyrant would kill him—but if he did bring back the Earthgirl, Meryola would have him executed. He was caught either way.

For once his nimble mind was snared. He shook his head moodily.

The girl was in the dungeon. The shadow of a plan began to form in his mind—a plan that might carry him on to success. He would need help, though. He would need an accomplice for this; it was too risky a maneuver to attempt to carry off himself.

The first step, he thought, would be to free the girl. That was all-important. With her dead, there was no chance for success.

Quickly he found the hall that led toward the stairs, and entered the gloomy, dark stairwell. He started downward, downward, around the winding metal staircase, heading for the dungeons where he had left the girl imprisoned.

There was a sound as of distant thunder coming from below. Someone running up the stairs, Hendrin wondered? He paused, listening.

The noise grew louder. Yes. Someone was coming.

Cautiously he stepped back into the shadows of the landing and peered downward, waiting to see who was coming.

He could see, on the winding levels below, the figure—the figure of an Earthman. *By Hargo,* he thought. *It's the one who tried to buy the girl from me— Archman! What's he doing here?*

Then the Mercurian thought: *he's shifty. Perhaps I can use him.*

He ducked back into the shadows and waited. A moment later Archman, breathless, came racing up the stairs. Hendrin let him round the bend, then stepped out of the darkness and seized the Earthman firmly.

Lon Archman stiffened tensely as the unknown attacker's arms tightened about his chest. He struggled to free his hands, to get at the zam-gun, but it was impossible. The assailant held his arms pinioned in an unbreakable hold.

He squirmed and kicked backward; his foot encountered a hard surface.

A deep voice said, "Hold still, Archman! I don't mean to hurt you."

"Who are you?"

"Hendrin. The Mercurian. Where are you heading?"

"None of your business," Archman said. "Let go of me."

To his surprise, the blue alien said, "All right," Archman found himself free. He stepped away and turned, one hand on his zam-gun.

The Mercurian was making no attempt at an attack. "I want to talk to you," Hendrin said.

"Talk away," Archman snapped.

"Where are you coming from? What are you doing in the palace, anyway?"

"I'm coming from the dungeons, where I was tossed by some of Darrien's tunnel guards. I'm escaping. Understand that? And as soon as I'm through telling you this, I'm going to blast a hole in you so you don't carry the word back to your master Darrien."

Surprise and shock were evident on the Mercurian's face. "Escaping? From Darrien?"

"Yes."

"Strange. From our brief meeting I thought you were loyal. Who are you, Archman?"

"That doesn't much concern you." He gestured impatiently with the zam-gun, but he was reluctant to blast the Mercurian down. It seemed that the blue man was concealing something that could be important.

There was a curious expression on the Mercurian's hard-shelled face, as well. Archman looked warily around; no one was in sight. He wondered just how, loyal to Darrien the Mercurian was…and if Hendrin could be used to further his own ends.

"I've just been talking to that girl you brought in here," he said. "What's she doing in the dungeons? I thought you were going to sell her to Darrien."

"I did. Darrien's mistress Meryola had a fit of jealousy and ordered the girl killed, while Darrien's back was turned."

"I see!" Archman now understood a number of things. "All's not well between Darrien and his mistress, then?" He grinned. "And you're the cause of the trouble, I'll bet."

"Exactly," said the Mercurian. "You say the girl's still in the dungeons alive?"

Archman nodded. "For the time being. She's locked in, but the jailer's dead. I killed him when I escaped."

"Hmm. I'm in a funny fix—Darrien wants me to get the girl back for him, or else he'll kill me—but if I return the girl Meryola kills me. It's a tight squeeze for me. I'm caught either way."

"I'll say." Plans were forming rapidly in Archman's mind. If he could get the girl out of the dungeon, and somehow manipulate her and this Mercurian, who was undeniably in a bad situation—

"Earthman, can I trust you to keep your tongue quiet?" Hendrin asked in sudden desperation.

"Maybe…maybe not."

"I'll have to take my chances then. But you're a renegade; I'll assume your highest loyalty isn't to Darrien but to yourself. Am I right?"

"You could be," Archman admitted.

"Okay. How would you like to have that girl for yourself, plus half a million credas? It can be arranged, if you'll play along with me."

Archman allowed a crafty glint of greediness to shine in his eyes, and said, "Is this a joke?"

"Mercurians generally play for keeps. I'm telling the truth. Are you interested? The girl, and half a million platinum credas."

"Who foots the bill?"

CHAPTER EIGHT

There was a long pause. Then Hendrin said, "Krodrang, The Overlord of Mercury. I'm in his pay."

A tremor of astonishment rocked Archman, nearly throwing him off guard. He mastered himself and said, "I thought you were one of Darrien's men. What's all this about Krodrang?"

Lowering his voice and peering cautiously around the stairs, the Mercurian said: "Krodrang is one who would usurp the power of Darrien. I'm on Mars for the purpose of killing Darrien and stealing his power. If you'll play along with me, I'll see to it that you get the girl—and Krodrang is not a poor man."

Archman was totally amazed. So there were *two* assassins out for Darrien's neck! *Well,* he thought, *between us we ought to get him.*

But as he stared at the Mercurian, he knew that killing Darrien would not end the job. Hendrin would have to go, too—or else he'd get back to Krodrang with the plans for the Clanton Mine, the orthysynthetic robots, and other of Darrien's secrets, and Earth would face attack from Mercury.

It would take delicate handling. But for the moment Archman had an ally working toward the same end he was.

"Well?" Hendrin asked. "What do you say?"

"Kill Darrien and collect from Krodrang, eh? It sounds good to me. Only—how are you going to get at Darrien? Those orthysynthetic robots—"

"Meryola knows which of the Darriens is real and which is a robot. And she's scared stiff that the Earthgirl's going to replace her in Darrien's affections. I've got an idea," Hendrin said. "We can play Darrien and Meryola off against each other and get everything we want from them. It's tricky, but I think you're a good man, Earthman—and I *know* I am."

He had the Mercurian's characteristic lack of modesty, Archman thought. The Earthman wondered how far he could trust the blueskin.

It looked good. As long as the Mercurian thought that Archman was simply a mercenary selling out to the highest bidder and not a dedicated Earthman with a stake of his own in killing Darrien, all would be well.

"Where do we begin?" Archman asked.

"We begin by shaking hands. From now on we're in league to assassinate the tyrant Darrien, you and I."

"Done!" Archman gripped the Mercurian's rough paw tightly.

"All right," Hendrin said. "Let's get down to the dungeon and free Elissa. Then I'll explain the plan I've got in mind."

In the musty, dank darkness of the dungeon level, Archman said, "She's in that cell—the third one from the left. But I don't know how to open it. There's a Martian in there with her."

"How did that happen?"

"They came to get me—Dorvis Graal wanted to question me on some silly matter, which is why I was being held here. I decided to make a break for it. The door was closing as I ran out. The girl and the Martian were trapped inside."

"And you couldn't get them out?"

"No," Archman said. "I couldn't figure out how to open the door again. I tried, but it was no go, so I started up the stairs. Then you caught me."

The Mercurian nodded. Suddenly he stumbled and grunted a sharp Mercurian curse.

"What happened?"

"Tripped on something." He looked down and said, "By the fins I'd say it's a Plutonian. His head's been blown off with a zam-gun."

"That's the jailer," Archman said. "I killed him when I escaped."

"He would have known how to open this damned lock, too. Well, I guess it couldn't be helped. Did you try blasting the door open with your gun?"

"Wouldn't work. The door heated up, but that was all."

Again the Mercurian grunted. He began to grope along the wall, feeling his way, looking for a switch. Archman joined him, even though in the murky darkness he could scarcely see. The Mercurian's eyes were much sharper. A Mercurian needed extraordinary eyes: they had to filter out the fantastic glare of the sun in one hemisphere, and yet be able to see in the inky gloom of Mercury's nightside.

"These doors work by concealed relays," Archman said. "There ought to be a switch that trips the works and pulls back the door. That Plutonian knew where it was."

"And so do I," Hendrin exclaimed. He extended a clawed hand into one of the darkest corners of the cell block and said, "There are four controls here. I guess it's one for each of these cells. I'm going to pull the third from the left, and you get ready in case that Martian makes trouble."

"Right."

Archman drew his zam-gun and stood guard. No sound came from within; he hoped Elissa was all right. She'd been left alone with that Martian for nearly twenty minutes now. Quite possibly the tusked creature had recovered consciousness by now. Archman hoped not.

"Here goes," Hendrin said.

He yanked the switch. The relays clicked and the door slid open.

Archman half expected the Martian to come charging out as soon as the door opened. He expected to be fighting for his life. He expected almost anything but what he actually saw.

The Martian was lying where he had left him, sprawled in the middle of the cell. Elissa, clad only in her single filmy garment, was squatting by the Martian's head.

As the door opened, the Martian stirred. Elissa coolly reached out, grabbed a handful of the alien's wiry skull-hair, and cracked the Martian's head soundly against the concrete floor of the cell. The Martian subsided.

Elissa looked up, saw Archman. "Oh—it's you."

"Yes. I came back to free you," he said. "I see you've been having no trouble with your friend here."

She laughed a little hysterically. "No. Every time he started to wake up, I banged his head against the floor. But I didn't know how long I could keep on doing it."

"You don't need to do any more," said Hendrin, appearing suddenly. "Archman, you'd better tie the Martian up so he doesn't give us any more difficulties."

At the sight of the hulking Mercurian, Elissa uttered a little gasp. *"You—!"*

"What am I going to tie him in?" Archman asked.

"You might tear my robe up into strips," Elissa suggested, bitter sarcasm in her voice. "I've been wearing clothing for almost an hour anyway."

"That's an idea," said the Mercurian coolly. "Yes— use her robe, Archman."

The Earthman chuckled. "I don't think she intended you to take her seriously, Hendrin. I'll use my shirt instead."

"As you please," the Mercurian said.

Elissa glared defiantly at both of them. "Who are you going to sell me to now?" she asked. "You, Hendrin— you've parlayed me into quite a fortune by now, haven't you?"

Archman realized that he had told the girl his true identity. Cold sweat covered him at the recollection. If she should give him away—

To prevent that he said quickly, "Say, Hendrin, the girl's had a raw deal. I suggest we tell her what part she plays in this enterprise right now."

"Very well. I'm sorry for the mistreatment I've given you," Hendrin told her. "Unfortunately you became part of a plan. I'm on Mars for the purpose of assassinating Darrien. I'm in the pay of Krodrang of Mercury."

"And I'm assisting him," Archman said hastily, nudging Elissa to warn her not to ask any questions. "We're both working to assassinate Darrien. You can help us, Elissa."

"How?"

"Hendrin will explain," Archman said.

"I'll help you only on one condition—that you free me once whatever plan you have is carried out."

Hendrin glanced at Archman, who nodded. "Very well," Hendrin lied. "You receive your freedom once the job is done." He smiled surreptitiously at Archman as if to tell him. *The girl will be yours. His name was hardly trustworthy.*

Archman rose. "There. He's tied. All right, Hendrin: explain this plan of yours, and then let's get out of here."

He faced the Mercurian eagerly, wondering just what the blue man had devised. Archman was a shrewd opportunist; he had to be, to handle his job. Right now he was willing to pose as Hendrin's stooge or as anything else, for the sake of killing Darrien. Afterward, he knew he could settle the score with Krodrang's minion.

"Here's what I have in mind," Hendrin said. "Darrien and Meryola are at odds over this girl, right? Very well, then. I'll take Elissa back to Darrien and tell him that—"

"No!" This from the girl.

"Just for a few minutes, Elissa. To continue: I'll take the girl to Darrien, and tell him that Meryola ordered her killed, and I'll make up enough other stories so Darrien will send out an order to execute Meryola. I think he's sufficiently smitten by Elissa to do that.

"Meanwhile, you, Archman—you go to Meryola and tell her what I've done. Tell her Darrien is going to have her killed, and suggest to her that if she wants to stay alive she'd better get to Darrien first. After that, it's simple. She'll tell you how to kill Darrien; you do it, we rescue Elissa, get Meryola out of the way somehow, and the job is done. Neat?"

"I couldn't have planned it better myself," Archman said admiringly. It was so. This was exactly as he would have handled the situation. He felt a moment of regret that he and Hendrin were working for opposite masters; what a valuable man the Mercurian would be in Intelligence!

But Hendrin would have to die too, for Earth's sake. He was a clever man. But so was Darrien, Archman thought. And Darrien would have to die.

"What about me?" Elissa asked. "Are you sure you'll get me out of this all right?"

Archman took her hand in his, and was gratified that she didn't pull away. "Elissa, we're asking you to be a pawn one last time. One more sale—and then we'll rid the universe of Darrien. Will you cooperate?"

She hesitated for a moment. Then she smiled wanly. "I'm with you," she said in a resigned tone.

CHAPTER NINE

Hendrin waited nervously outside the throneroom with the girl. "You say Darrien's in there, but not Meryola?" he asked the unsmiling guard.

"Just Darrien," the guard replied.

"The stars are with us," Hendrin muttered. He took the girl's arm and they went in.

Together they dropped on their knees. "Sire!"

Darrien rose from the throne, and an expression of joy lit his warped little face. "Well, Mercurian! You've brought the girl—and saved your life."

"I did it not to save my life but my honor," Hendrin said unctuously. "Your Majesty had accused me of acting in bad faith—but I've proved my loyalty by recovering the girl for you."

Darrien came waddling toward them on his absurdly tiny legs and looked Elissa up and down. "You've been in the dungeons, my dear. I can tell by the soot clinging to your fair skin. But by whose order were you sent there?"

Hendrin glanced at the courtiers, who maintained a discreet distance but still were within hearing. "Sire, may I talk to you a moment privately?"

"About what?"

"About the girl…and Meryola."

Darrien's sharp eyes flashed. "Come with me, then. Your words may be of value to me."

The dwarfish tyrant led Hendrin into a smaller but equally luxurious room that adjoined the throneroom. Hendrin stared down at the tiny Darrien, nearly half his height. Within that swollen skull, the Mercurian thought, lay the galaxy's keenest and most fiendish mind. Could Darrien be manipulated? That was yet to be seen.

One thing was certain: this was not the real Darrien before him. The tyrant would not be so foolish as to invite a massive Mercurian into a small closed room like this; it would amount to an invitation to assassinate him.

"Sire, the girl Elissa was in the dungeons at the direct order of the lady Meryola."

"I suspected as much," Darrien muttered.

"And when I arrived there, I found that the jailer was about to carry out an order of execution on Elissa, also at your lady's behest."

"What?"

Hendrin nodded. "So strong was the order that I was forced to kill the jailer, a worthless Plutonian, to prevent him from carrying out the execution."

"This is very interesting," Darrien mused. "Meryola rightly senses a rival—and has taken steps to eliminate her. Steps which you have circumvented, Hendrin." Gratitude shone in Darrien's crafty eyes.

"I have further news for you, Sire. When you came upon me in Meryola's chambers earlier today—it was not an errand of perfumery that brought me there."

"I hardly thought it might be."

"On the contrary—your lady was pleading with me— to *assassinate* you."

Darrien—or the Darrien-robot—turned several shades paler. Hendrin reflected that the robot, if this were one, was an extraordinarily sensitive device.

"She said this to you?" Darrien asked. "She threatened my life?"

"She offered me five thousand credas. Naturally, I refused. Then she offered me her body as well—and at this point, you entered the room."

Darrien scowled. "My life is worth only five thousand credas to her, eh? But tell me—had I not entered the room, Mercurian, would you have accepted her second offer?"

"I was sorely tempted," Hendrin said, grinning. "But pretty women are easily come by—while *you* are unique."

"Mere flattery. But you're right; Meryola has outlived her worth to me, and I see now that I'll have to dispose of her quickly," Darrien reached for the speaking-tube at his elbow. "I'll order her execution at once—and many thanks to you for this information, friend Hendrin."

Archman paused for a moment outside the door of Meryola's private chamber, preparing his plan of attack and reviewing the whole operation so far.

He'd been in and out of trouble—but Darrien was going to die. The mission would be accomplished. And Lon Archman would survive it.

He had a double motive for survival now. One was the simple one of wanting to stay alive; two was the fact that he now thought he had someone to stay alive *for.* Perhaps.

He knocked gently at the door.

"Who's there?"

"You don't know me, but I'm a friend. I've come to warn you."

A panel in the door opened and Archman found himself staring at a dark-hued eye. "Who are you from, Earthman? What do you want?"

"Please let me in. Your life depends on my seeing you."

A moment passed—then, the door opened.

"Are you the lady Meryola?"

"I am."

She was breathtakingly lovely. She wore but the merest of wraps, and firm breasts, white thighs, were partially visible. There was a soft, clinging sexuality about her, and yet also a streak of hardness, of coldness, that Archman was able to appreciate. He also saw she was no longer very young.

She was holding a zam-gun squarely before his navel. "Come in, Earthman, and tell me what you will."

Archman stepped inside her chambers. She was nearly as tall as he, and her beauty temporarily stunned him.

"Well?"

"Do you know Hendrin the Mercurian, milady?"

"Indeed. Are you from him?"

"Not at all. But I know Hendrin well. He's a cheating rogue willing to sell out to any bidder."

"This is hardly news," Meryola said. "What of Hendrin?"

He eyed her almost insultingly before answering. Meryola was indeed a desirable creature, he thought— but for one night only. Archman mentally compared her with Elissa Hall, who was nearly as beautiful, though not half so flashy. It wasn't difficult to see why Darrien preferred Elissa's innocence to this aging, shrewd beauty.

He smiled. "At this very moment," he said, "Hendrin is with our master Darrien. He has brought him the girl Elissa, and they are together now."

"It's a lie! Elissa's in the dungeons!"

"Would you care to call your jailer, milady?"

She stared suspiciously at him and picked up the speaking-tubs. After nearly a minute had passed, she looked back at Archman. "The line's dead, Earthman."

"As is your jailer, Hendrin freed the girl and took her to Darrien. And one other fact might interest you: Darrien has tired of you. He has made out the order for your death."

"*Lies!*"

Archman shrugged. "Lies, then. But within the hour the knife will be at your throat. He vastly prefers the younger girl. Believe me or not, at your peril. But if you choose to believe me, I can save your life."

"How, schemer?"

At least she would listen.

He moved closer to her, until he was almost dizzied by her subtle perfume. "You hold the secret of Darrien's robots. Reveal it to me, and I'll destroy Darrien. Then, perhaps, another Earthman will claim your favors. Surely you would not object to ruling with me."

She laughed, a harsh, indrawn laugh, and it seemed to Archman that the cat's claws had left their furry sheath. "You? So that's your motive—you ask me to yield Darrien's secret in order to place yourself on the throne.

Sorry, but I'm not that foolish. You're an enterprising rascal, whoever you are, but—"

Suddenly the door burst open. Three Martians, their tusks gleaming, their thick lips drawn back in anticipation of murder, came rushing in.

"Darrien's assassins!" Archman cried. He had his zam-gun drawn in an instant.

The first Martian died a second later, complete astonishment on his face. A bolt from Meryola's gun did away with the second, while a third spurt finished the remaining one. Archman leaped nimbly over the bodies and fastened the bolt on the door.

Then he stooped and snatched a sheet of paper from the sash of one of the fallen Martians. He read it out loud: "To Grojrakh, Chief of the Guards: My displeasure has fallen upon the lady Meryola, and you are to dispatch her at once by any means of execution that seems convenient. D."

"Let me see that!"

He handed her the paper.

She read it, then cursed and crumpled the sheet. "The pig! The pig!" To Archman she said, "You told the truth, then. Pardon me for mistrusting you—"

"It was only to be expected. But time grows short."

"Right." Her eyes flashed with the fury of vengeance. "Listen, then: none of the Darriens you have seen is the real one. There are three orthysynthetics which he uses in turn. Darrien himself spends nearly all his time in a secluded chamber on the Fifth Level."

"Is the room guarded heavily?"

"It's guarded not at all. Only I know how to reach it, and so he sees no reason to post a guard. Well, we'll give him cause to regret that. Come!"

"Down this hallway and to the left," Meryola said.

This was the moment, Archman thought. It was the culmination of his plan and the ending of a phase of history that traced its roots to a politician's pompous words years ago—"*Let Venus be our penal colony*—"

So they had planted the seeds of evil on Venus, and they had banished Darrien there to reap them. And with the destruction of Darrien's empire on Venus, they had permitted Darrien to escape and found yet another den of evil.

The end was near, now. With Darrien dead the mightiest enemy of justice in the galaxy would have been blotted out. And Darrien *would* die—betrayed by his own mistress.

They reached the door.

It was a seemingly plain door, without the baroque ornamentation that characterized the rest of the palace. And behind that door—Darrien.

"Ready?" Meryola asked.

Archman nodded. He gripped the zam-gun tightly in one hand, pressed gently against the door with the other, and heaved.

The door opened.

"There's Darrien!" Meryola cried. She raised her zam-gun—but Archman caught her arm.

Darrien was there, all right, crouching in a corner of the room, his wrinkled face pale with shock. He wore a strange headset, evidently the means with which he controlled the orthysynthetics.

And he held as a shield before him—

Elissa.

This was one pleasure the tyrant had not been willing to experience vicariously through his robots, evidently. Tears streaked the girl's eyes; she struggled to escape Darrien's grasp, without success. Her flesh was bloodless where his fingers held her. There was no sign of Hendrin.

"Let me shoot them," Meryola said, striving to pull her arm free of Archman's grip.

"The girl hasn't done anything. She's just a pawn."

"Go ahead, Archman," Darrien taunted. "Shoot us. Or let dear Meryola do it."

Meryola wrenched violently; Archman performed the difficult maneuver of keeping his own gun trained on Darrien while yanking Meryola's away from her. With two guns, now, he confronted the struggling pair at the far end of the little room.

"Shoot, Archman!" Elissa cried desperately. "I don't matter! Kill Darrien while you have the chance."

Sweat beaded Archman's face. Meryola flailed at him, trying to recover her weapon and put an end to her lord and her rival at once.

The Earthman held his ground while indecision rocked him. His code up to now had been, the ends justify the means. But could he shoot Elissa in cold blood for the sake of blotting out Darrien?

His finger shook on the triggers. *Kill them,* the Intelligence Agent in him urged. But he couldn't.

"The Earthman has gone cowardly at the finish," Darrien said mockingly. "He holds fire for the sake of this lovely wench."

"Damn you, Darrien. I—"

Meryola screamed. The door burst open, and Hendrin rushed in. Right behind the Mercurian, coming from the opposite direction, came one of Darrien's orthysynthetic duplicates—Darrien's identical twin in all respects, probably summoned by Darrien by remote control.

And the orthysynthetic carried a drawn zam-gun.

What happened next took but a moment—a fraction of a moment, or even less.

Meryola took advantage of Archman's astonishment to seize one of his two zam-guns. But instead of firing at Darrien, she gunned down Hendrin!

The Mercurian looked incredulous as the zam-gun's full charge seared into his thick hide, crashing through vital organs with unstoppable fury.

Meryola laughed as the blue Mercurian fell. "Traitor! Double-dealer! Now—"

The sentence was never finished. The zam-gun in the hand of Darrien's double spoke, and Meryola pitched forward atop Hendrin, her beauty replaced by charred black crust.

Archman snapped from his moment of shock, and his gun concluded the fast-action exchange. He put a bolt of force squarely between the orthysynthetic's eyes, and a third body dropped to the floor.

From behind him came a cry. "Archman! Now! Now!"

He whirled and saw, to his astonishment, that Elissa had succeeded in breaking partially loose from Darrien. Archman's thoughts went back to that moment in Blake Wentworth's office when, in a drug-induced illusion, he had won the right to participate in this mission by gunning down a Martian across the vast distances of the red desert. His marksmanship now would count in reality.

His finger tightened on the zam-gun.

"You wouldn't dare shoot, Earthman!" Darrien said sneeringly. "You'll kill the girl!"

"For once you're wrong, Darrien," Archman said. He sucked in his breath and fired.

A half-inch to the right and his bolt would have killed Elissa Hall. But Archman's aim was true. Darrien screamed harshly. Archman fired again, and the tyrant fell.

He found himself quivering all over from the strain and tension of the last few moments. He looked around at the grisly interior of the room. There lay Hendrin, the shrewd Mercurian, who had played one side too many and would never live to collect his pay from Krodrang. There, Meryola, whose beauty had faded. There, the Darrien-robot. And there, Darrien himself, his foul career cut short at last.

"It's over," he said tiredly. He looked at Elissa Hall, whose lovely face was pale with fear. "It's all over. Darrien's dead, and the mop-up can begin."

"Your aim was good, Archman. But you could have fired at Darrien before. My life doesn't matter, does it?"

His eyes met hers. "It does—but you won't believe that, will you? You think I'm just a killer. All right. That's all I am. Let's get out of here."

"No—wait." Suddenly she was clinging to him, "I— I've been cruel to you, Archman—but I saw just then that I was wrong. You're not just the murderer I thought you were. You—you were doing your job, that's all."

He pulled her close, and smiled. He was thinking of Intelligence Chief Wentworth, back on Earth. Wentworth had rated Archman's capabilities at 97.003%. But Wentworth had been wrong.

Archman had done the job. That was 100% efficiency. But he had Elissa now too. Score another 100%. He gently drew her lips to his, knowing now that this mission had been successful beyond all expectation.

THE END

If you've enjoyed this book, you will not want to miss these terrific titles…

ARMCHAIR SCI-FI & HORROR DOUBLE NOVELS, $12.95 each

D-21 **EMPIRE OF EVIL** by Robert Arnette
THE SIGN OF THE TIGER by Alan E. Nourse & J. A. Meyer

D-22 **OPERATION SQUARE PEG** by Frank Belknap Long
ENCHANTRESS OF VENUS by Leigh Brackett

D-23 **THE LIFE WATCH** by Lester del Rey
CREATURES OF THE ABYSS by Murray Leinster

D-24 **LEGION OF LAZARUS** by Edmond Hamilton
STAR HUNTER by Andre Norton

D-25 **EMPIRE OF WOMEN** by John Fletcher
ONE OF OUR CITIES IS MISSING by Irving Cox

D-26 **THE WRONG SIDE OF PARADISE** by Raymond F. Jones
THE INVOLUNTARY IMMORTALS by Rog Phillips

D-27 **EARTH QUARTER** by Damon Knight
ENVOY TO NEW WORLDS by Keith Laumer

D-28 **SLAVES TO THE METAL HORDE** by Milton Lesser
HUNTERS OUT OF TIME by Joseph E. Kelleam

D-29 **RX JUPITER SAVE US** by Ward Moore
BEWARE THE USURPERS by Geoff St. Reynard

D-30 **SECRET OF THE SERPENT** by Don Wilcox
CRUSADE ACROSS THE VOID by Dwight V. Swain

ARMCHAIR SCIENCE FICTION CLASSICS, $12.95 each

C-7 **THE SHAVER MYSTERY, Book One**
by Richard S. Shaver

C-8 **THE SHAVER MYSTERY, Book Two**
by Richard S. Shaver

C-9 **MURDER IN SPACE** by David V. Reed
by David V. Reed

ARMCHAIR MASTERS OF SCIENCE FICTION SERIES, $16.95 each

M-3 **MASTERS OF SCIENCE FICTION, Vol. Three**
Robert Sheckley, "The Perfect Woman" and other tales

M-4 **MASTERS OF SCIENCE FICTION, Vol. Four**
Mack Reynolds, "Stowaway" and other tales

If you've enjoyed this book, you will not want to miss these terrific titles…

ARMCHAIR SCI-FI & HORROR DOUBLE NOVELS, $12.95 each

D-91 **THE TIME TRAP** by Henry Kuttner
THE LUNAR LICHEN by Hal Clement

D-92 **SARGASSO OF LOST STARSHIPS** by Poul Anderson
THE ICE QUEEN by Don Wilcox

D-93 **THE PRINCE OF SPACE** by Jack Williamson
POWER by Harl Vincent

D-94 **PLANET OF NO RETURN** by Howard Browne
THE ANNIHILATOR COMES by Ed Earl Repp

D-95 **THE SINISTER INVASION** by Edmond Hamilton
OPERATION TERROR by Murray Leinster

D-96 **TRANSIENT** by Ward Moore
THE WORLD-MOVER by George O. Smith

D-97 **FORTY DAYS HAS SEPTEMBER** by Milton Lesser
THE DEVIL'S PLANET by David Wright O'Brien

D-98 **THE CYBERENE** by Rog Phillips
BADGE OF INFAMY by Lester del Rey

D-99 **THE JUSTICE OF MARTIN BRAND** by Raymond A. Palmer
BRING BACK MY BRAIN by Dwight V. Swain

D-100 **WIDE-OPEN PLANET** by L. Sprague de Camp
AND THEN THE TOWN TOOK OFF by Richard Wilson

ARMCHAIR SCIENCE FICTION CLASSICS, $12.95 each

C-31 **THE GOLDEN GUARDSMEN**
by S. J. Byrne

C-32 **ONE AGAINST THE MOON**
by Donald A. Wollheim

C-33 **HIDDEN CITY**
by Chester S. Geier

ARMCHAIR SCI-FI & HORROR GEMS SERIES, $12.95 each

G-9 **SCIENCE FICTION GEMS, Vol. Five**
Clifford D. Simak and others

G-10 **HORROR GEMS, Vol. Five**
E. Hoffmann Price and others

If you've enjoyed this book, you will not want to miss these terrific titles...

If you've enjoyed this book, you will not want to miss these terrific titles…

ARMCHAIR SCI-FI & HORROR DOUBLE NOVELS, $12.95 each

D-111 **THE MOON ERA** by Jack Williamson
REVENGE OF THE ROBOTS by Howard Browne

D-112 **SON OF THE BLACK CHALICE** by Milton Lesser
SENTRY OF THE SKY by Evelyn E. Smith

D-113 **OUTPOST ON THE MOON** by Joslyn Maxwell
POTENTIAL ZERO by S. J. Byrne

D-114 **OUTPOST INFINITY** by Raymond F. Jones
THE WHITE INVADERS by Ray Cummings

D-115 **TIME TRAP** by Rog Phillips
THE COSMIC DESTROYER by Alexander Blade

D-116 **THE OTHER SIDE OF THE MOON** by Edmond Hamilton
SECRET INVASION by Walter Kubilius

D-117 **DANGER MOON** by Frederik Pohl
THE HIDDEN UNIVERSE by Ralph Milne Farley

D-118 **THE WAILING ASTEROID** by Murray Leinster
THE WORLD THAT COULDN'T BE by Clifford D. Simak

D-119 **THE WHISPERING GORILLA** by Don Wilcox
RETURN OF THE WHISPERING GORILLA by David V. Reed

D-120 **SPECIAL EFFECT** by J. F. Bone
WARLORD OF KOR by Terry Carr

ARMCHAIR SCIENCE FICTION CLASSICS, $12.95 each

C-37 **THE GREEN MAN RETURNS**
by Harold M. Sherman

C-38 **THE SHAVER MYSTERY, Book Five**
by Richard S, Shaver

C-39 **MARS CHILD**
by Cyril Judd

ARMCHAIR MASTERS OF SCIENCE FICTION SERIES, $16.95 each

MS-7 **MASTERS OF SCIENCE FICTION AND FANTASY, Vol. Nine**
Poul Anderson, "The Star Beast" and other early tales

MS-8 **MASTERS OF SCIENCE FICTION, Vol. Ten**
Robert Moore Williams, "???" and other tales

If you've enjoyed this book, you will not want to miss these terrific titles…

ARMCHAIR SCI-FI & HORROR DOUBLE NOVELS, $12.95 each

D-121 **THE GENIUS BEASTS** by Frederik Pohl
THIS WORLD IS TABOO by Murray Leinster

D-122 **THE COSMIC LOOTERS** by Edmond Hamilton
WANDL THE INVADER by Ray Cummings

D-123 **ROBOT MEN OF BUBBLE CITY** by Rog Phillips
DRAGON ARMY by William Morrison

D-124 **LAND BEYOND THE LENS** by S. J. Byrne
DIPLOMAT-AT-ARMS by Keith Laumer

D-125 **VOYAGE OF THE ASTEROID, THE** by Laurence Manning
REVOLT OF THE OUTWORLDS by Milton Lesser

D-126 **OUTLAW IN THE SKY** by Chester S. Geier
LEGACY FROM MARS by Raymond Z. Gallun

D-127 **THE GREAT FLYING SAUCER INVASION** by Geoff St. Reynard
THE BIG TIME by Fritz Leiber

D-128 **MIRAGE FOR PLANET X** by Stanley Mullen
POLICE YOUR PLANET by Lester del Rey

D-129 **THE BRAIN SINNER** by Alan E. Nourse
DEATH FROM THE SKIES by A. Hyatt Verrill

D-130 **CRY CHAOS** by Dwight V. Swain
THE DOOR THROUGH SPACE By Marion Zimmer Bradley

ARMCHAIR SCIENCE FICTION CLASSICS, $12.95 each

C-55 **UNDER THE TRIPLE SUNS**
by Stanton A. Coblentz (single) 1950s, Fantasy Press

C-56 **STONE FROM THE GREEN STAR**
by Jack Williamson, Amazing 10 & 11/31, (cleared by Eli)

C-57 **ALIEN MINDS**
by E. Everett Evans

ARMCHAIR SCI-FI & HORROR GEMS SERIES, $12.95 each

G-13 **SCIENCE FICTION GEMS, Vol. Seven**
Jack Vance and others

G-14 **HORROR GEMS, Vol. Seven**
Robert Bloch and others

If you've enjoyed this book, you will not want to miss these terrific titles…

ARMCHAIR SCI-FI & HORROR DOUBLE NOVELS, $12.95 each

D-131 **COSMIC KILL** by Robert Silverberg
BEYOND THE END OF SPACE by John W. Campbell

D-132 **THE DARK OTHER** by Stanley Weinbaum)
WITCH OF THE DEMON SEAS by Poul Anderson

D-133 **PLANET OF THE SMALL MEN** by Murray Leinster
MASTERS OF SPACE by E. E. "Doc" Smith & E. Everett Evans

D-134 **BEFORE THE ASTEROIDS** by Harl Vincent
SIXTH GLACIER, THE by Marius

D-135 **AFTER WORLD'S END** by Jack Williamson
THE FLOATING ROBOT by David Wright O'Brien

D-136 **NINE WORLDS WEST** by Paul W. Fairman
FRONTIERS BEYOND THE SUN by Rog Phillips

D-137 **THE COSMIC KINGS** by Edmond Hamilton
LONE STAR PLANET by H. Beam Piper & John J. McGuire

D-138 **BEYOND THE DARKNESS** by S. J. Byrne
THE FIRELESS AGE by David H. Keller, M. D.

D-139 **FLAME JEWEL OF THE ANCIENTS** by Edwin L. Graber
THE PIRATE PLANET by Charles W. Diffin

D-140 **ADDRESS: CENTAURI** by F. L. Wallace
IF THESE BE GODS by Algis Budrys

ARMCHAIR SCIENCE FICTION & HORROR CLASSICS, $12.95 each

C-58 **THE WITCHING NIGHT**
by Leslie Waller

C-59 **SEARCH THE SKY**
by Frederick Pohl and C. M. Kornbluth

C-60 **INTRIGUE ON THE UPPER LEVEL**
by Thomas Tempel Hoyne

ARMCHAIR SCI-FI & HORROR GEMS SERIES, $12.95 each

G-15 **SCIENCE FICTION GEMS, Vol. Eight**
Keith Laumer and others

G-16 **HORROR GEMS, Vol. Eight**
Algernon Blackwood and others

A POWER THAT SIGNALED EARTH'S POSSIBLE DOOM

Randolph Warren wasn't trying to destroy himself and his whole lab with his new scientific apparatus, but that's what almost happened. What Randolph had been laboring on was a revolutionary experiment relating to the energy of matter. However, what he actually accomplished was the total annihilation of matter, transmuting it into a sheer, raw atomic force, the likes of which had never been known before. Properly developed, it promised to be a boon to mankind. But a small syndicate of the world's wealthiest energy brokers— who weren't afraid to wreak death and destruction—set their sights on this amazing new discovery. Soon Warren and his associates found themselves flung outside the known Universe—beyond the end of space. The only question that remained was could they return to their own space and time before Earth fell prey to a group of power-hungry madmen?

CAST OF CHARACTERS

DR. RANDOLPH WARREN
To say he was brilliant was the understatement of the century, but could he live long enough to appreciate his own brilliance?

DONALD M. PUTNEY
His love of science and his own vast wealth made him the perfect patron to a scientific project that might change the world forever.

THADDEUS E. NESTOR
A wealthy businessman with big ambitions. Unfortunately his lust for wealth and power outweighed his sense of right and wrong.

DR. JAMES ATKILL
His reputation as a brilliant scientist was preceded only by his reputation as a dirty rotten scoundrel.

BURT HILLEN
He and his mob were considered vital to the establishment of a new world order. Vital, yet…disposable.

WILSON
Smart and fairly competent he was, even occasionally creative. His main problem was he liked to talk a little too much.

THOMAS BLAMEN
Working with a renowned physicist on an amazing experiment was a true thrill—but it got him a lot more than he bargained for.

BEYOND THE
END OF SPACE

By
JOHN W. CAMPBELL

ARMCHAIR FICTION
PO Box 4369, Medford, Oregon 97504

CHAPTER ONE

"HOLD 'er there for a while, Tom. I want to get three more electroscopes and a recording bolometer. The thermopile doesn't record, you know. The recording electroscope will give us a photographic record—but no immediate information as the experiment progresses," called Dr. Randolph Warren. He swung himself to the three-inch thick fused quartz tube, wrapped his hands around its milky column, and slid down the shaft forty feet to the ground below. A whining hum of electric motors and the slap-slap-slap of the silk ribbons mounting to the huge aluminum sphere above, drowned out the call of Tom Blamen, inside the sphere. Tom wanted to know if he might try the thing on low voltage once. Tom didn't get an answer, but he looked at the meters, and saw a needle quivering at the point marked "17" on the master meter.

"17,000,000—and I'll have to discharge somehow before he can place the ladder to climb back. It's a shame to waste all that—" He looked out of his observation window, a conducting window made of two sheets of plate glass separated by a layer of dilute sulfuric acid. Set in the aluminum sphere it maintained the conductivity of the metal across the gap.

Twenty-five feet away a weird mushroom rose from the concrete floor of the concrete laboratory. Set on a tripod of carefully designed insulators, the half-sphere seemed some strange growth. The polished aluminum with its discharge points pitted and scarred by the lashing force of terrific discharges was joined to the sphere by a clear tube of fused quartz. This seemed swollen half-way between, and the three-inch tube opened to the size of a football. Around this swelling, held in position by strings of insulators depending from the ceiling twenty feet above, were three tremendous magnets. The swelling in the tube contained a smaller globe or sphere and in this was a filament of iron wire. The inner tube was very highly evacuated, one of the dozen tubes Sanderson brought back with him from his voyage to space beyond the Earth's atmosphere in fact. In 1952 there had been a dozen tubes, now in 1955, only three years later, but four remained, so those absolutely evacuated tubes were very valuable. Opened, then sealed while in empty space, they were the only *EMPTY* tubes on Earth. It spoke of the importance of this experiment that the University had permitted this tube to be used.

Blamen's gaze shifted back to the mushroom tower, down its insulated base to the powerful electric motor that drove a white ribbon of silk. The ribbon of silk brushed against a bit of *CHARGITE,* a specially designed compound that gave the silk a charge of electricity. The endless belt whisked the charge up to the sphere above, where points collected it and carried it away to the sphere. Like an endless-chain bucket conveyor the silk ribbon was bringing electric charges up, as a similar ribbon carried equal—but opposite charges to the control sphere where he sat.

Tom Blamen was in a whirl of hesitancy and doubt. He looked nervously about. He could discharge the spheres in a bolt of lightning to the heavy metal conductors thirty-five feet away by simply running out the discharge-arms. But it seemed a waste of energy—

Ran Warren was back—he stood in the door looking up at the man in the window of the sphere.

"Shall I discharge through the tube?" asked Blamen, eagerly.

Warren didn't hear, but as anyone might, nodded in annoyance. "Yes—discharge to towers—send down the ladder, of course."

Blamen accepted it as authority to do what he wanted. He gave a glance at the dials—17.6 million volts now. He stopped the motors, and the bands slowed with a doleful slap-slap-slap. He threw another switch, and the three enormous magnets surged with terrific, hitherto unused, power, a magnetic field of compressive force, three tremendous magnetic fields opposing each other, and pressing down simultaneously on that little inner tube. The fine iron filament-wire trembled. Suddenly it burst into blazing, explosive incandescence as a tremendous current rushed through it—and simultaneously the terrific, stored energy at 17.6 million volts smashed through the iron vapor in the little tube. Seventeen and six tenth millions of volts leaping across a gap of eight inches! Warren leaped forward in amazed surprise. "Tom, you fool—don't—" He stopped, and froze as a terrible cry came to his ears.

In the tube a light had formed. The discharge was all over—should have been. But in the tube was a virulent thing that glowed some indescribable color, a violet so tremendously deep that it seemed a red-black. A wave of energy struck Warren that made him throw a protective hand across his eyes, and stagger back from that room of incandescence, back, and out to the corridor beyond. His eyes were in torture, his whole body felt crisp and dry. Still that terrific light was glowing around the corner of the door, beating out at him, and still the feeling of heat and some terrible impact of energy parched his body. There were faint mutterings, shakings and quivers in the building now, the light from within was growing stronger. Suddenly there was a terrific explosion. The light grew bluer, and more brilliant, it seemed to increase rapidly, and the man staggered under a wave of beating, destroying energy, invisible, but terribly tangible.

Then in an instant it was over, and only a heaving and restless movement of the building remained. Warren slumped to the floor as cries of panic echoed from other parts of the Heavy Apparatus Laboratories.

A crowd of men was collected about him, a doctor bending over him and two stretcher bearers nearby, when he regained consciousness. He groaned in agony as he woke. His whole body was stiff and sore. He could feel a terrific coat of sunburn over its entire surface except where something as thick as his belt or shoes had protected him.

"Burn—radiation burn of some kind. Take him to the infirmary and coat him with 732-aE. It's serious. How's the other man?"

"Dead—very. Burned raw, and looks as though he might have been electrocuted first. We'd better clear out, the wall is cracked badly."

"Wh—what happened?" asked Warren blankly and inanely.

"If you don't know, nobody can tell you, Warren," replied Jordan of Chemical Processes, who stood beside him now. "You started an earthquake though that darned near knocked the building down. We all left, then discovered you two hadn't, and came back. You were lying here, and Blamen—he's gone, Ran," he concluded gravely.

"Blamen—started the tube—something happened. I called him and told him to discharge to the towers—to the ground—but he discharged through the tube. Is the apparatus all right?" Warren asked anxiously.

"The Sanderson Tube is gone—everything else O.K."

Warren groaned. "Oh Lord, I could replace anything but that!"

The stretcher bearers were carrying him away before he got a chance to say any more, and the pain of the burns came back. He groaned softly. "The Sanderson tube!"

*   *   *

"And so, Putt-putt, I've come to you as usual. It was a wild yarn I told, and I was dismissed with regrets, but my illness, lasting more than three months, made it imperative for them to have some man to take my place in the meantime—and somebody said something about a Sanderson tube and somebody else mentioned 175,000 dollars damages to buildings—

"And now I've told you how I left the University."

Donald Murray Putney, (sometimes referred to by Warren as "Putt-putt" and "filthily rich") inventor of the gasoline turbine, which had promptly wrecked several hundred promising gasoline engine companies, till they bought his patents, and supplied Warren with material for endless annoyance, was not satisfied that he heard the whole story.

"Yes, how—but not, why. What was the wild tale?" he demanded. Putney knew Warren was not addicted to wild tales, especially if they might be interpreted as excuses for himself.

"Well—I suggested that the action, which I saw, must be due to some hitherto unknown, force. Certainly, Don," he went on, warming up to his subject, "there wasn't enough energy in my apparatus, taking the total energy stored on the two spheres, the field energy of the three magnets, and the potential energy, too, for that matter— they fell down you know—to start an earthquake. Also, a discharge, even of 17.6 million volts—all the instruments jammed—wouldn't give me a case of sun or radiation burn that would lay me up in the infirmary for three straight months. Anyway—I had different aims." He quieted suddenly as he remembered he was started again, and the last reception of his theory had made it a painful discussion for him.

"What were the aims?"

"Energy of matter," replied Warren grimly.

Putney was silent for some moments, puffing his pipe leisurely as he leaned back in his chair. The furnishings of his bachelor apartment were dedicated to the Goddess of Comfort.

"Hmmm—that would cause an earthquake. In fact it might well cause several dozen earthquakes. It would certainly cause an earthquake on Wall Street.

"By the way, who led the laughter in the Directors Meeting?"

"Old Nestor," replied Warren guardedly. "And it surprised me a lot. Naturally I would be surprised anyway, but old Nestor is no dumb business man. He got on that faculty for more reasons than one."

"Yes," agreed Putney, "he did." Putney smiled sourly. "That old boy is a live man, and alive to the opportunities too. He bought in there, because he can get information cheap and wholesale. That's why Nestor Aircraft is a strong investment. And does Nestor love me—? He does—like a shark would. I nearly wrecked him with that little patent of mine, and he hasn't gotten over it yet. What did he say?"

"He started them off, perhaps. I didn't expect him to say 'Impossible' but he was the first."

"Oh—did he?" Putney smiled to himself. "And has he spoken to you since? Warren, I learned when I had patents to sell—and you know I've sold a lot more since that turbine affair—that Nestor has ideas of his own on business manners. Who gets the rights on the discovery if you remain with the University?"

"Why—they would!" exclaimed Warren.

"Uh-huh—open to everybody to use. No money in that. Well, you're kicked out. If your ideas are correct, who gets the rights now?"

"I would—"

"And that's where you're wrong. Would you? How could you get them—how could you prove it—how could you build the apparatus—?" Putney leaned forward with blazing black eyes. "You know you couldn't—not till Nestor furnished your laboratory, and he'd run off with the patents, and you'd get a salary. You're black-listed with Universities now, and you know it. So does he. He saw that you had millions—billions perhaps, in the palm of your hand. So he fired you. In a day he'll offer you a laboratory job, and set you on that again, and he'll get the money."

Warren gazed at his friend in amazement. "You're right, Putt-putt. You're damn right. Only I'm going to ask you into a partnership with me. You've got the money, and I've got an idea, that is apparently worth Nestor's time."

Putney stood up and stretched forth his hand. "And we've got a partnership, Ran, that nothin'll bust!"

CHAPTER TWO

"MR. NESTOR will see you now, sir," the secretary said. She smiled pleasantly at the tall, powerfully built, gray-eyed man. She began to wonder, as she noticed the expression about his eyes and mouth, just how successful Mr. Nestor would be in this interview. Mr. Nestor was usually successful in his interviews, but there were little humorous crinkles around the big man's eyes, and graven lines of power and intelligence. And the jaw was powerful, the clean, square-cut lines of the face and the set of the head on broad powerful shoulders indicated determination. Most indicative of all, the lips were tight-pressed and they looked unpleasant. She mentally shrugged her shoulders, very pretty shoulders she knew they were too, and stood aside for him to pass.

"Ah, Dr. Warren, I'm glad to see you again," said the shrewd old man. The mechanical smile was intended to be winning. Ran Warren didn't like it. He didn't like Nestor for that matter, for it was Nestor, in his younger days, who had changed his career. Pressure here, influence there—and his father began to yield, for he had never had the determination and the power of will of his mother. Then five big men, and one man—who was going to be big—jumped on him, and his holdings began to slide rapidly. But it made Nestor.

"What was it you wanted to see me about, sir?" asked Warren, attempting to come to the point.

"I have been wondering since I spoke so hurriedly in the Advisory Meeting, whether that idea of yours might not have been right. It really does seem strange to me that so serious a result could have followed a mere discharge in a tube. What do you believe caused the earthquake?" The keen, black eyes twinkled up at him like the eyes of a bird.

"Radiations, sir. I am certain no such power as would move the Earth's crust was ever developed in those little electric motors that accumulated the discharge. I believe that that discharge started a release of the energy of matter, that the radiations were very largely of an extremely short wavelength, and that they penetrated the building readily. Certainly you know that all the photographic material in the laboratory was ruined, and some was at a considerable distance, behind walls. Suppose the radiations penetrated through the ground, and into the layers below. Eventually they would be absorbed. At whatever point they were absorbed, we would know there was water, for the laboratory was on made land. That water, converted to steam, would certainly have some such result. The radiations were so powerful in all probability that they passed through me, and the other humans without hindrance, and hence without result."

Nestor's eyes were bright. There was a calculating gleam behind them. "That's an interesting theory, and quite possible—if you really did succeed in smashing the atom."

"But I didn't. I destroyed it. It wasn't merely broken, it was annihilated, I believe."

"Matter cannot be destroyed, I thought?" said Nestor sharply.

"Apparently the others agreed with you. Were you going to reinstate me at the University?"

"I'm afraid that can't be done, Dr. Warren. But I was interested enough to ask you if you would like a job with my research staff. You could continue your experiments if you wished. I can offer you fifteen thousand a year."

A slow smile dawned on Warren's lips. "I'm afraid you are mistaken, Nestor. If you investigate the State files, you'll find there's a new firm—Putney and Warren, Research Engineers. I think you'll have to get someone else, so I'll say—goodbye."

Warren turned and strode out. Mr. Thaddeus Eustace Nestor looked after him with amazement. "What—hey— come back—" But Warren had already left. Nestor began to curse, then stopped abruptly. His plans had gone badly awry. He had intended to snap up Warren before anyone else could, and as Putney had suggested, get the benefit of this inconceivably important discovery. Now to his horror he discovered that not only was he unable to get it, but instead of getting it himself, Warren was to get the benefit. Had he left Warren in his position at the University he would at least have had an equal share in the discovery with all others, but now he certainly would not. There was just one answer.

He pressed a button, and presently the secretary appeared. "Send Mr. Williams over, Miss Oliver." The secretary retired and called Mr. Robert Williams, head of the Nestor Research Laboratories.

Nestor Aircraft was only one of T. E. Nestor's holdings. The man had forward-looking ideas, and he had long since realized that research would pay an income as well as any other business, and the Laboratories were simply his invention factories. They handled all sorts of problems, and Mr. Williams was the head, and a physicist.

He appeared in a few minutes, and went into Nestor's soundproof office. "Well, what is it?"

"I told you Warren was coming on board? Well, he isn't. I made a mistake." Williams grinned broadly. The Old Man had made a mistake, and a bad one evidently. He didn't look happy, and Williams had been informed that morning that he was about to be made Assistant Director of Research, with Warren as Director. It hadn't appealed to him.

"A mistake? What was it?" he asked ironically.

"I got that blasted scientist loose from the University so he could come here—and what does he do? Does he thank me for it and come?—no! He's started a firm of his own. And Williams, get this; he's discovered how to annihilate matter."

Williams started and looked at Nestor seriously.

"How do you know?"

"Read about the explosion at the University three months ago? That was it. A tiny piece of iron wire, he said."

"Where do I come in?"

"You're going to duplicate his apparatus, and better his record. I've already got track of a Sanderson tube."

"You're mistaken. I'm going to do nothing of the kind. Warren is the greatest atomic man in the world, and he always was a fool for luck. Remember the time Canstanti tried to start his racket on the University and sent a bomb? It fell beside Warren, and turned out a dud. Well, I'm not superstitious, but if it killed one man and nearly killed him, then it's bad medicine for Mrs. Williams' little boy, Bobby.

"What do you know about the power he used, voltages, currents and so forth? Suppose that instead of the slow release that merely killed one and half killed another, besides causing an earthquake, we got a rapid release. Any idea what would happen? You could blow this old world clear across the solar system!"

"You won't handle it? Why not try it with just a little?"

"Little? 'There ain't no sich animile' as the hick said. If I worked under a microscope I'd still have enough to blow the whole city off the map. I know physics plenty good for my work, but I'm no second Warren. You know his latest work has been showing Einstein's mistakes. There's just one other man who might do it, and that's Jimmy Atkill."

"Atkill—he's a disreputable crook. They won't even publish his papers anymore."

"Sure he's a crook—but they never proved he killed the old bird. He had some kind of a death ray, and they never proved he used it. Try and convince a jury of twelve good men and dumb, that a death ray they can't even show in evidence did the job!"

"He's a crook—but he's brilliant. Try him."

"All right. If you're afraid."

Williams grinned. "That's not a dig. That's not fear either, it's common sense. Want to play with matches in a dynamite plant? Want to come out and watch me work on that idea, when a piece that you can't even see under a microscope would blow the whole city off the map?" The Physicist shook his head and left.

Nestor took out a pocket chess set, and sat playing chess with various combinations and problems. Then, after nearly half an hour, he put his little set away and reached for the telephone.

"Miss Oliver, get the physicist, Dr. James Atkill, on my phone. I don't know where he is, nor in what city. Get him," Then he hung up and went back to his papers. It was nearly an hour before Miss Oliver announced that Dr. Atkill was on the wire.

"Dr. Atkill speaking; is that Mr. Nestor?"

"Yes. Where are you?"

"Detroit."

"Be here in an hour and I've got a big job for you. Hop by nearest plane. I'll give orders to send you right through. I'm in New York."

"I've got a good job here. What have you got, how long will it last, and how much?" was Dr. Atkill's response.

"Read about the earthquake at the University here three months ago? That was some of Randolph Warren's work. Destruction of the indestructible. That's all I can say over the telephone. The salary will be agreeable. Will you come?"

There was a soft whistle over the wire. "So my old friend Ran Warren has been shaking down buildings—and the indestructible has been destroyed. And why isn't Warren working on it?"

"Fool! He is. That's why I said hurry."

"Doesn't take much apparatus if he's working on it. He always was poor as the proverbial church mouse," chuckled Atkill.

"Doesn't it? Putney's backing him. Once and for all, are you coming?" demanded Nestor irritably.

"On my way, gran'pa!" Nestor's face went red at this rejoinder from Dr. Atkill, and his close-cropped gray hair seemed to stand up stiffer than usual. He started to splutter into the microphone, but the instrument was mockingly dead.

CHAPTER THREE

"WELL, from the expression on your face, I should say that my guess as to friend Nestor's ideas was right, Ran?" grinned Putney as Warren came into the laboratory. Half a dozen men of Putney's staff were grouped around their chief, and smiled at the angry Warren.

"Very," replied Warren with a grimace. "He offered me fifteen whole thousands a year—and he knows damn well that, if my ideas are right, the thing is worth—oh there isn't any possible limit to set on it. It's beyond value. And the old skunk would keep it tightly wrapped up in his own private pink ribbon—to be sold only at his own prices. He'd probably put it just low enough to wreck the existing power companies, and high enough to make an ungodly profit."

"What do you think his next move will be?"

"Lord, Putt, I don't know." Warren looked at his friend in blank surprise." I hadn't thought. What will he do?"

"He'll call in Williams, his chief of laboratories, and tell him to go ahead on it. And Williams, being an intelligent though not highly scrupulous man, will decline without thanks, explaining to Nestor just why it won't be safe. Nestor will either force him to do it, or get—I think he'll get Atkill, he's probably the next best man."

"He's the best, the best physicist in the world, and one of the most interesting men, but has the moral sense of a feudal baron. 'I want it. It's mine'. That's his one and only code. Nestor will probably be gypped. It's a shame a brilliant man like Atkill can't behave."

"He's second best—you're best and you know it. Now let's forget that and see what we want. You have the notes on your experiment?"

"Why no, they belonged to the University," exclaimed Warren.

"Nut! We don't know whether Nestor's got 'em or not." Putney pulled out a handkerchief and wiped a light glistening of perspiration from his brow. "Wilson," he said, looking at one of his staff members, "you go to the University and try to buy them. I'll pay for them, up to a million—and the remains of the apparatus that was wrecked." Wilson nodded, and started off at once. Putney sat in silence for some time.

"I wonder—I wonder if Nestor might not try to get in here, and acquire some data?" asked Warren softly. "May I borrow your men for a while?"

"Go to it, Ran. What's the idea now?"

"Watch—and we may show you some new ideas." The physicist turned to the men around him. "Come on men, this is going to be war."

The rest of the staff had gathered, a score of men in all. To a man they were with Putney, and everyone of that scientific staff were with the great physicist in his research. To them, the idea of the energy of matter was a fire to stimulate them to the utmost.

Outside the laboratory Warren surveyed the grounds with an appraising eye. The laboratory building stood on a low hill. Behind rose ridge upon ridge of the rolling New Jersey hills. The Kittatiny range off to the Northwest crowned the view with a green-blue ribbon. Below the large, concrete building was a series of smaller sheds and houses. The kitchen and mess-hall were set over a clear, bubbling spring; a little stream of water trickled down from it to the clear lake below.

The hillside itself was clear, but covered with out-cropping rocks. Behind the sheds and the main laboratory tall metal towers strode off across the hills to the super-power transmission line five miles away. A high metal fence surrounded the entire property.

"Our first job is to set up a number of burglar alarms, and a burglar catcher or two. Men, you all live here don't you? I have reason to suspect we aren't going to have a happy stay while we are developing this thing, so we're going to fix it so no one can get in or get out again without our knowing it. Come on…"

For the rest of that day the men worked, while Wilson—with the supply-plane—made numerous trips to and from New York and the surrounding towns, bringing food and other supplies. One of the things Putney ordered was a complete gasoline-driven power plant. The power line was too accessible, and since there had been no reason to believe it would fail he had never had an auxiliary plant.

The entire grounds of the laboratory were crossed and re-crossed with an endless chain of beams of ultra-violet light, and photoelectric detectors. A capacity bridge was attached to the metal fence, and several others set up in the grounds, making it impossible for anyone to approach them, without giving the alarm. Then the fence was wired, and it was possible to turn the current on either the power line or the power plant into it at any time.

It was night before they finished, and the hundreds of invisible beams stretched their fingers about. The grounds were equipped with searchlights that would automatically turn to the section from which any alarm came, and flood it with light. Three men were sent out to make an attempt to steal across the grounds, knowing perfectly the distribution of the beams, and with a careful map of the grounds. It could not be done. The beams could be avoided only by coming within range of the capacity bridges, and instantly a blinding glare flooded them, and the tortured shriek of a siren announced their failure.

Air attack likewise proved impossible, for again the capacitances were disturbed. "I think," said Warren with a broad smile, "that we are safe."

"Uh-huh—Atkill came to see Nestor today," answered Putney.

"Then you were right again. Williams didn't like the job."

"When do you start work?" asked Putney.

"Tomorrow—when I've had some sleep," replied Warren instantly. "Let's turn in."

After breakfast they settled down once more to the discussion. Wilson was present, his combined office of scientific assistant and stenographer making him useful. Wilson was a small, slightly grayed man, self-effacing and one of those people who are merely useful, but not much more. He'd never had an original idea, and probably never would, but as a scientific amanuensis, he was invaluable.

"What apparatus are you going to need, Ran?" asked Putney. "That's the point to start on."

"To begin with, the remains of my old apparatus, and a dozen pencils, the integraph, several calculus books, and some tables of natural and ten-base logs. Also some reference books on field theories might help. In the meantime, I'm going to discuss the idea with you. Wilson, will you see if you can get those things together?"

"Yes, Dr. Warren. In the study?" At Warren's nod he set off at once.

"Now, Putt, this is the theory I was working on when the grand smash came. I firmly believe that it is a law of nature that matter cannot be destroyed. Nothing in this universe can possibly destroy it."

Putney stared at him in amazement. "Wha—what happened then?"

"Matter was destroyed, and released its energy!" There was a twinkle in Warren's eyes as he, replied.

"All right. I give up. What's the answer?"

"I said, and I believe, that matter cannot be destroyed in *this* universe. The matter that was destroyed was *not* in this universe! That matter was suddenly hurled beyond the end of space, out of space altogether, beyond the fourth-dimensional surface of our three dimensions. This universe is a hollow fourth-dimensional hyper-sphere, and the universe as we know it is the surface of that sphere. Well, what happens if it escapes from that sphere altogether?"

"But—it can't!" objected Putney.

"But—if it did?" demanded Warren.

"It—it could—it *couldn't exist!* Good lord man, is that the secret! It *can't* exist, it is automatically thrown into a condition that prohibits its existence!" Putney's incredulous eyes fixed themselves on Warren.

"Almost, but not quite. That's true to an extent, that's what would happen if I could project it *completely* out of all spaces, but the thing is, at the instant it was projected out of this universe, it would itself become the center of a new hyper-space. Mass in itself creates a space about it. Do you see my point?"

"Right."

"Then that can't be done. But I *can* project it into a space whose laws are such that the matter *can't* exist. And the point where that other space touches ours, there the two modify each other and intercommunicate. Energy released in one can be tapped from the other. I threw my energy into the alien space, and it is destroyed to free energy. That energy comes back to this space, and is at once converted to such a form of energy as is capable of existence in this space. Do you see the operation?"

Putney's face was pale as he contemplated the titanic forces that worked on the bit of matter that had been annihilated in Warren's apparatus. Space! Space, the master of Forces and Energies, space, with its immutable and infrangible laws had done Warren's bidding, and brought him the prepared result! A bit of matter tossed to it! A digested and refined bit of energy thrown back in its stead.

"Right! But, man, how can the thing be done, why, doesn't it slip off of itself? How did you know there would be such a space near—near the surface of our world, as would do that?"

"There doesn't have to be. I *make* that bit of space. Don't you see, Putt, it *does* slip through of itself, tries to build itself a new space, and perhaps does, but where the terrific forces I'm sending through with it are, even that other space of its creation is so affected as to be sharply curved. Remember, Earth's gravity is leaking through too, and so is the intense magnetic and electrical force. That maintains the conditions I want—or did, for some lucky reason. I must know exactly what the forces were. They told me that when Blamen was hit, every meter froze, the pivots melted, the works were blown out by something. Even the great magnets I used were melted after a time.

The increase in the power of the magnets must have been the reason for the rapid increase in the intensity of the radiation that I had a chance to notice.

"At any rate, I'm going to work on them now, and I think I'd better learn something. I had the world's luckiest break really. You know I was trying to disturb space. I thought I might succeed in transmuting that iron wire. I never expected to annihilate it. If it had gone up all at once—you would probably have been annihilated as well. Did you stop to think that if I had started the experiment, as I intended, I would have been killed instead of Blamen—or rather with him? I never could blame the old boy too much!"

Warren went to the study with Putney, and together they started the work on the field strengths and data they had, the effects they knew or imagined or had learned, and tried to make sense. Little by little the chips of darkness fell from the truth, and they began to perceive the facts.

CHAPTER FOUR

SOMEBODY told me," said Dr. James Atkill, "that you were clever, Nestor. That somebody was all wet, as the saying went. You ought to judge men better. You might have known that Warren would never fall for that play of yours, not while he had a friend like Putney to go to.

"Then, not content with that, you let him walk the apparatus right out from under your nose. My Lord, I didn't think they made 'em so dumb. Now, he's got all the data and all the notes and all his own memories. Were there any pictures of the apparatus?"

"Yes," snapped Nestor angrily, "and I have all of them." This tall, lean physicist with his disconcertingly keen gray eyes and the easy air of mockery, a subtle feeling that he was laughing at you even though his face was serious, rattled the shrewd old man.

"Well, that'll do some good. Did you get any of the apparatus-mechanics who set up his stuff? Those mechs will know something about it." He ruffled his wavy blond hair thoughtfully.

"No. I haven't gotten them, but—"

"But your laboratory staff needs an increase," interrupted Atkill. "Get 'em."

"All right. I'll send for them now." The financier pushed a button, and told Miss Oliver of the increase in the laboratory staff. Half an hour later she told him the men had agreed.

"Now," went on Atkill, "just what happened?"

"Well—nobody really knows, you see—"

"I see—I see that everyone but Warren was out of the way, and so he is the one man on earth who saw it done. My dear employer, could you think of any way to mess things up any more? I'm the best physicist in the world, but when you start me off with a handicap like that, I haven't a very good chance. The one living man who saw it, the man who made the apparatus, and the man who has the instruments that record the experiment—all the one man, and one of the brightest little boys loose. Now what miracle is it you want?"

"Could I help it? It wouldn't have done me—that is us—any good if he had stayed with the University would it?"

"No, but if you'd had the brains God gave little red ants, you could have gotten something for yourself by offering him a *real* reward. But when you turned him loose on the world—"

"But let's stop this and see what we know. He had some of the high-tension generators such as they were using at M.I.T. back in '30, larger of course, and better, but the same idea. This—" he stared at the photograph Nestor had tossed him, "is evidently a quartz tube, with the electrodes in it. How'd he turn the voltage into them—it takes a tricky switch to handle 25,000,000 volts?"

"I don't know, that's something you'll have to figure out. He was going to patent that," said Nestor.

"That's all right then, he'll have given the data to the University. He invented and perfected it while he was with them, and he'll be fool enough to turn it over even though you did discharge him.

"Then the Sanderson tube apparently—ah here it is. Between the big magnets. Anything special about them—no I guess not. Just unusually powerful.

"Lord—Nestor, get on that phone quick, and corner every existing Sanderson tube. If he needs them, he'll be held up forever, if we have all the tubes going!"

"That's an idea—that's helpful!" Nestor turned to the telephone, and in five minutes had the laboratory cornering the only other perfect vacuum on Earth. There was a ship preparing to leave for the Moon with a large expedition, but it would be a year or more before they'd be back, and by that time the battle would have been won—or lost. Their tubes wouldn't help Warren any.

"Why did he need one?" asked Nestor.

"Matter you imbecile—destruction of matter. He can't start that in the midst of matter and not have it blow up everything within miles of the place. He has to have a perfect absence of matter."

"Somebody told me that he had an iron wire in there," objected Nestor.

"Certainly. I know it. There were twelve tubes, one had a platinum wire, one had iron, one had gold, and so on. And they all had platinum electrodes. But the question is did he use that iron wire? Or was it just there? I think he used it because of the magnets—and there isn't another tube with iron in existence—damn!" The physicist looked at the picture thoughtfully and ruffled his hair. "Well, he can't get it either. But he may not need it now."

"I—eh—wonder if we couldn't—eh—buy the data and instruments from—somebody?" suggested Nestor nervously.

"Yes. I thought of stealing them too," returned Atkill frankly. "It would be much easier to say what you mean."

He smiled pleasantly at the sharp-faced old man. "But I don't think it will be easy. Putney's no fool, and neither is my revered colleague, Warren. I'll bet they have so many ultra-violet beam thief-detectors around there that you can't wiggle an eyebrow without starting a siren. We'll find out. His men all live there, so we can't get at them to give us a few hints."

"I believe a man named Wilson comes to town occasionally for supplies. He has one of our transport planes."

"We might try him. I don't know him, what's he like?"

"He's about fifty, slightly gray, rather stoop-shouldered, and always looks disappointed," replied Nestor thoughtfully.

"Thumb-nail directory. That's excellent, he won't be disappointed longer. I'll see him. In the meantime—"

He was out of the office before Nestor could say anything further. Nestor wanted him to sign a contract. He hadn't had a chance to talk to him about that. But neither was Atkill satisfied, and he was back as suddenly as he had left.

"By the way, I want one hundred thousand win or lose, and ten million dollars down if I succeed before Warren," he announced.

"*What! Ten Million!* Get out! You won't have a sniff!" Nestor cried. He meant to roar it, but his voice was too high-pitched to roar effectively.

"And whom will you get instead?" asked Atkill, smiling pleasantly, "and likewise what will I do with the information I already have?"

"Nothing!" snapped Nestor.

"Plenty," replied Atkill gently. "I'll sign a contract with you at that figure."

Half an hour later he did, and went off to talk with the apparatus mechanics from the University who had arrived in the meantime. He started them at once building a static generator of the necessary power. Then he took the nearest moving platform and headed East across the city. Twenty minutes later he was inquiring among the speakeasies selling the illegal 10% drinks. He had several that were considerably over that figure, met several old acquaintances, and finally found the man he wanted.

Joe Keller was not a prepossessing figure. He was small, about five-feet-three in height, and weighed less than 130 pounds. His eyes were very black and never rested long on the same point; his black hair was constantly falling over his eyes in unruly tangled strands. A stubble of two-days' beard covered his cheeks and his thin, weak jaw. His clothes had fitted perfectly, but they were mussed and wrinkled now.

"'Lo, Atty. Whatcha wan'?" Keller's then lips were permanently glued together, and seemed never to move, only the cigarette, at one corner of his thin, straight mouth, bobbed slightly, and the trails of smoke waved about in the heavy air of the cheap rented room.

"Little job, Joe. What brings you to this hovel?"

"Sompin' new in the worl'," announced the little man looking with disgust at his surroundings. "I used rubber gloves on a vault, and they hadda thing what ate holes in the rubber. Lef' muh fingers all over the place, an' didn't know it till I took the gloves off. Too damn late then. They're lookin'. I can't do nothin' now."

"No, but your enforced seclusion doesn't prevent your comrades from doing something does it? Why not let them go out, say to the Putney laboratories, and I think they'll find some things there I want. I might pay as much as fifteen grand for them."

Keller sat up with a start. "What things?"

Minutely Atkill described the instruments, and the notes that he wanted. He said they would probably be in some sort of safe, but that might be overcome. A little XY-321 would help too, he intimated, and could be obtained from him. The XY would put anyone in the laboratory building to sleep for three hours, unless he had a special mask, or unless the windows were open. XY required a high concentration but was fairly effective then. Inside a house it was perfect.

"Gotcha. Come 'round tomorra," said Joe Keller. Atkill pursued his way to the West, and then back to the Nestor offices.

CHAPTER FIVE

IN the big, bare, concrete room a score of men were working at a peculiar apparatus that rose rapidly from the floor. There were two towers capped by great aluminum spheres. Their stilt-like legs were made of fused quartz, and electric motors were being installed at the base of the towers.

In another room, two men were working alone. Warren and Putney, fighting calculations that staggered their abilities, and ideas that staggered their imaginations.

"I think," said Warren, his eyes shining as he stared hard at the latest result, "we aren't going to need a Sanderson tube at all this time. According to that all I need do is vary the V factor in 254 here slowly, and I won't need a very high vacuum. Shall we try it?"

"We won't try it any other way," Putney reminded him sourly. "Nestor beat us to it on the Sanderson tubes, as you know."

Warren laughed happily. *"Stung!* We didn't need 'em. But we *do* need those static generators there. We can control the thing now, we know how it can be controlled, and we can draw power from that energy center in the form we want here once it's started, and after that we'll never need to worry! Except to find other facts about its properties.

"Lord! Putney—these sheets—they hold the secret of the energy man has sought since the atom was discovered! Before us lie the equations that are the key to the infinite

energy, the energy that will banish work from Earth! And banish distance too! I'm sure this field here represents the annihilation of the gravity curvature in space!" he exclaimed, pointing to a brief expression that represented in fact the second great secret.

"But, Putt, these others, these things that suddenly become irreducible and immutable, these end-equations when we attack one set of unknowns with given values. Some I recognize; here's the Planck formula, derived from space-curvatures! Here's magnetic forces, here electrostatic fields—but man, what is this one? It's like nothing I know, and these others—here's a formula for creating vibrational fields in space with any period of vibration up to the limiting period of Millikan rays. Can we try these?"

"We can try them—with an automatic machine," replied Putney, "when the machine is a hundred million miles from Earth."

"I think that'd be the best idea. Well, it's dark now, and time for us to stop."

They went at last for supper, and then after a brief talk on ways and means of using any power, they turned in.

It was well into the night when Warren leaped out of bed with a cry of surprise and pain. Something had stung him, and for a moment he did not know what it was. A similar muffled cry came through the wall from Putney's room an instant later, and Warren, now wide awake, smiled. The thick walls stopped most of the sound, but he could guess what Putney was doing. The capacitance alarm signal had warned them that someone was approaching the fence, and brought them out of bed with a jump.

As the mild shocking current wakened them, the room lights were turned on automatically.

"Putt—how many are there?" asked Warren as he came into Putney's room. There was a small television set here, and the screen was glowing brightly, but a peculiar colorless and misty scene was represented. The screen was portraying the section of the fence that had been affected. Someone was attempting to approach unseen. It seemed ridiculous to see the man crouching here and there, and peering over stones and skulking in non-existent shadows. Powerful lights were flooding the grounds with *"brilliant"* ultra-violet beams. They were so short as to be beyond vision, but so long as to have very slight fluorescent effects, and the three men were utterly ignorant of the blazing lights.

"Shall we let them in?" asked Putney.

"Why not?" asked Warren with a laugh. "They're trying the gate!"

Putney had pushed the secondary alarm that brought the men to his room, and they were appearing now with pistols and rifles, clad in pajamas or hastily donned trousers.

"We're letting 'em into the grounds," explained Putney as the men stared at the screen. "They'll hit one of the ultra beams sure, and start a siren howling. If they don't run for it then, especially when the visible light strikes them, I miss my guess."

"They're through," whispered someone.

"They cut the lock out with an atomic hydrogen flame."

The three separated. One stayed at the gate, holding it open against the spring that tended to close it, a revolver in one hand. The other two started softly for the house.

"They'll hit the arbor-hangar beam," estimated Kennet, the laboratory electrical apparatus specialist.

"The stone-pile inductance will spot them first," contended Wheeler, chief chemist.

The argument was interrupted by a sudden loud clicking from the master boards behind the screen. Suddenly a brilliant white pencil appeared on the screen spotting the two men and simultaneously a horrific wail shrieked from a huge siren. The three men froze instantaneously, then the two turned and beat a hasty retreat.

Putney had adjusted something before him. Now he threw a switch. The man at the gate gave a cry of pain and bounded back from the fence. The released gate suddenly swung to with a clang. It could not lock, however. The two running men hit the fence about the same time, and they too bounced back with a cry of pain. The fence was charged.

Putney threw a second switch with a grin, then a third. As he threw the second, the fence suddenly began to spit long streamers of flame, and miniature lightning bolts reached out, lapping at the ground and streaming up to the heavens.

The last switch had connected a microphone, and now as the wail of the siren died protestingly into silence, a monstrous voice issued from speakers on the laboratory.

"I would advise you to refrain from assaulting the fence. It might bear unhappy consequences. May I invite you gentlemen into the laboratory? If you will go to the spot of light thrown by the searchlight, you will be directed along the path."

The men walked sullenly to the light. Three unhappy, shabby looking specimens of humanity they were. Presently they were instructed to lay down their weapons, and proceed to the house without armaments.

"The reception committee decided to meet you here instead of at the gate," smiled Putney as the three came into the room, heavily guarded.

"What did we touch off?" growled the least washed of the three.

"Well, in the first place, when you approached the fence, the alarm got us out of bed, and turned on the flood lights," began Warren.

"Open-space!" sneered the leader. "We'd a' seen lights an' beat it."

"Look out—the entire grounds are flood-lighted," replied Putney waving to the screen, and the dark window. "Only it's dark light."

The men looked puzzled. They also looked unhappy.

"What did you men come here for?" demanded Warren.

"See if we c'u'd get yah and the fly-cops outta bed."

"I think they don't mean to answer, Putt," said Warren soberly, turning to his friend. "We'd better take them down to the laboratory and the infra-compressor till they become more talkative."

A gleam of laughter came into Putney's eyes. "Why not start them on the vibrator?"

"All right. Take 'em down, men." Three very worried crooks heavily guarded by ten husky scientist-mechanics were taken down to the laboratory.

"I don't think it's fair to use the vibrator on 'em without giving 'em another chance to talk." Kennet turned a compassionate eye on the invaders.

"Oh, I dunno. They knew what was comin' when they came here, and besides, it doesn't always cripple them. I remember the first time they used it the thing broke down about fifteen seconds, and the guy could walk within two weeks."

"Hey, guy, wat is dis ting?" asked the smallest of the captives. His voice was very hard—and slightly strained.

"Well, they attach electric things to your arms and legs," invented Kennet rapidly, "and they turn on a current that sorta slowly fires you inside, and makes you jerk and vibrate so your bones come out of the joints, and—but you'll see it pretty soon." Again that compassionate eye swept them.

They reached the main laboratory door, and Kennet told the others to hold them here while he went in. In a moment Putney and Warren appeared, and rapidly Kennet sketched his invention.

Ten minutes later the captives were brought in. A heavy wooden chair painted a glossy black was set beside a huge mass of compact apparatus. As they entered Putney threw a switch, and with a tremendous crackling, sparks five feet long began leaping from one contact to another. The humming deepened, and the sparks became steady roaring flame. Heavy chains hung over the chair, and some great thick cables stretched from the apparatus, ending in straps of soft copper.

"Put the big one in it first," ordered Warren, cocking his head and looking at him. "He'll last longer."

The big one attempted to resist, but was soon seated and chained in the great wooden, straight backed chair. Close behind his ears was that dull, powerful hum, and the roar and snap of vicious sparks that weirdly lit the laboratory with a flickering blue flame.

"Say, Warren, why not give the guy another chance before you start? He'll be crippled afterwards and may not be able to talk for a while," suggested Kennet.

"I—I'll talk—I'll talk," agreed the man in his fright. Accompanied by the hum and the crackle of sparks, lit by their flickering flame, the man talked fast and he talked truthfully. He didn't like the feel of heavy copper bands on his wrists, and the sound of snapping sparks. His account was detailed and vivid.

He had been sent to get any papers or notes he could find about the study, a map of which he had been given. Meanwhile his companion would attempt to locate and abstract the instruments that Atkill had described. They were to be taken to a certain junk shop, where someone would call for them. That was all he knew. The others ardently agreed.

"What'll we do with 'em?" asked Kennet finally when Warren had asked all the questions he wanted.

"Oh, send them back. We haven't any use for them."

It was three hours later when "Sporty" Cantoli reported to Joe Keller, announcing that his three men had come back badly scared, and convinced that they had escaped by a narrow margin from the fiends of hell. They had told everything they knew, and described vividly the torture they had undergone. Sporty reported he had not succeeded in getting anyone else to do the job.

CHAPTER SIX

"HELLO, Gramps," grinned Atkill as he came into the sedate, carefully furnished office of Thaddeus Nestor. "I've been making inquiries, and a friend of mine tried to steal those things, or have them stolen. Three men went, but Putney's no fool, as I said, and he had the whole place lit up with ultra-violet floodlights, and the men didn't even know they were walking under brilliant lights. They watched my friends come across the yard, and finally captured them. They've wired the big fence with A.C. evidently, for when they touched it they just bounced off again. Looks as though we'll have to work through Wilson if at all. Maybe he can give us some plans of the fortifications."

"In the first place," Nestor snapped irritably, "I'm not your grandfather—praise the good Lord—and in the second place I don't like this sending thieves. Did they tell anything?"

"Did they talk?" Atkill smiled faintly. "Did you think Putney wouldn't make them? He strapped 'em in a big wooden chair and set up a Tesla coil behind their ears. Loud noises, big sparks, spectacular display—and heavy copper conductors strapped on their wrists. I'll bet they talked so fast a dictaphone couldn't keep up." Atkill smiled faintly. "But don't worry, they didn't know anything anyway—or they'd have had the sense to carry a fluorescent screen of some sort to warn them. I asked a friend and he asked a friend of his and the friend of his confidentially told a friend of his, who sent three of his men. Besides, Putney knew who sent them without asking, anyway. Nobody else wants the junk."

"Well then, see the trouble you've gotten us into at the start!" wailed Nestor. "What can we do?"

"What can they do?" laughed the physicist. "They can't prove a thing. As a matter of fact they have made it impossible to send any of Joe Keller's friends. The whole gang is so scared now they wouldn't talk about it above whispers. I've got to hand it to that boy, Putney. Police protection wouldn't stop those crooks, but the 'muscle' they've got now stops every one of them.

" 'Muscle'? What's that?" Nestor inquired blankly.

"Reputation for unpleasant happenings." Atkill smiled engagingly. "In the meantime I've made some progress. My apparatus is started. And I think I know what Warren was trying to do."

"What?"

"Transmutation."

"Yes, of course. Is that the best your famous brain can do? Anyone over at the University could have told you."

"Yes, that's the best I can do right now. You ask one of your University friends exactly what Warren's theory of transmutation was. If he can't tell you, I will." Atkill started for the door, and called over his shoulder as he left, "But it doesn't work that way, so we can't make gold. I'm going to work."

Nestor looked suddenly interested, as Atkill mentioned transmutation, but his face fell as he was assured it wouldn't work. He growled some unintelligible remark, then picked up his desk telephone and called a number at the University. Presently he was speaking to Professor William Boyd.

"Hello, Professor Boyd?"

"Yes, is this Mr. Nestor?"

"Right. Say, do you know what Warren was working on when he ruined that apparatus?"

"It wasn't Warren who ruined the apparatus, Mr. Nestor, but his assistant, Blamen. But they were working on the transmutation of the atom. He hoped to change the nuclear structure."

"Uh-huh, so I heard. Do you happen to know what this hyp—hypothenuse was?"

"I can't say, he didn't tell anyone. I'm sorry, but why don't you ask him?"

Nestor growled, and hung up, and Boyd left the telephone with a gesture of distaste.

Atkill had found out where Wilson usually ate when he was in town for purchasing supplies, and had set a man to watch for him on his next trip into the city. Nearly a week went by, and Atkill was growing nervous. His apparatus had been finished, as best he could make it, and the Sanderson tube connected. However, it had a nickel wire instead of the iron wire Warren had used, and he was not at all sure what his results would be. Two tentative, low-voltage discharges in the tube had merely resulted in a peculiar feeling of strain in the laboratory, a feeling of some terrific jerk.

The mechanics had assisted him in making his apparatus, and had directed the work really, for they had seen the original mechanism Warren used in his successful, if not over-successful experiment. But they did not know that Warren had sent a current through the little iron wire, and Atkill did not guess this, for though the filaments had been sealed in all the tubes, they were practically never used, there was so seldom any reason for them. Sanderson had put them there in case they should be wanted, for it would be impossible to insert them after the tube was brought to Earth.

That, and the fact that Atkill was afraid, with reason, to try any high voltage on his tube, made his experiments unsuccessful. Further, his magnets were not properly arranged. Warren had changed them after the photograph Atkill worked from had been taken.

But when at last his scout reported that Wilson was entering the little restaurant, Atkill left his laboratory at once and hurried over to meet the little man.

He found him seated in one of the small private booths, a waiter hovering near. It was one of the old-fashioned restaurants where waiters served the customers, as Atkill knew. This particular waiter was in his pay, however.

Wilson glanced up as Atkill entered. "Dr. Atkill!" he exclaimed as he recognized the famous physicist.

Wilson agreed with Nestor's description. He had a disappointed look. Atkill was anxious to change that.

"Hello Wilson, may I join you?"

"Certainly, Doctor. I didn't think you'd know me, though I naturally knew you."

"Oh, I've seen you around." Atkill's smile was friendly, it seemed to intimate that Wilson was an equal, and a man he was glad to be friendly with. "And then too, I've used that clever little micro-spectroscope of yours."

Wilson glowed with satisfaction. His one invention, a slight improvement on an existing device, was a thing very dear to him. Atkill had won him over completely.

Half an hour later they left the restaurant the best of friends. Atkill had spread himself to be agreeable, and Wilson had talked a great deal more than he realized. Atkill had a perfect map of the complete defenses of the Putney laboratory, and knew exactly where to find the notes when he got in. However, he decided to send someone else. He couldn't afford to be captured.

"That fence—clever! Bet Warren thought of the capacitance bridge. But we can overcome that with a little patience. A bridge of our own, and a little static apparatus—" Atkill began planning just what sort of a thing would be needed to neutralize the effects of a man's capacity on the fence. He set to work on it soon after he reached the laboratory, and in a few hours had a suitcase that would contain his apparatus, within it the assembled machine was ready for use. He tried it on a metal plate set up against the wall, and the results gave perfect success. He could walk to the plate leisurely, and touch it without so much as disturbing the sensitive capacitance bridge.

He put his apparatus in the office safe, took down his hat, and shrugged on his coat after carefully washing up. He was smiling contentedly as he walked toward the moving way on Fifth Avenue Third. He threw away his cigarette, and stepped upon the third level escalator, paid his fare, and started toward the information point.

He found Joe in a little cottage on the Palisades. Joe was nattily dressed now, and looking happy. His cottage was entirely automatic, and heavily armed. The police, moreover, were no longer looking for him. He had grown a new set of finger prints.

Joe didn't greet him so enthusiastically this time. The last visit had resulted in rather unhappy consequences for some of his friends. "Hello Atty. Watcha want?" he asked apathetically.

"I'll tell you, Joe. I want to make an offer," began the physicist frankly. "I want a certain job done, it's going to be a bit difficult, perhaps, but it will be worth it to me, and

I'll make it worth it to you. I'll not give you any money for it." Joe looked puzzled, but not deeply so. He wasn't really interested, he had an excellent idea what the job was.

"Nah? What then?"

"The Death Ray machine—with sixty charges still in it."

Joe sat up like a spring coming into position. He stared at Atkill sharply, then slumped unhappily. "Now I know it can't be done. What is it? What y're getting at?"

"Oh, Joe, it can be done easily enough—now. You remember that place where those friends of yours went, and came back with tales of all sorts of things—terrible things—? Well, I found out a lot about that place from a man named Wilson, who works there, and Wilson told me all about it. You know, those rats of yours started spouting without so much as a slight burn! They're dirty liars, Joe. Wilson saw it, and he told me that all Warren did was to clamp them in a big wooden chair, and start a spark machine, what we call a Tesla Coil, about as dangerous as a fly-swatter, right behind their ears. It looks bad, and those rats got scared, and talked so fast they couldn't understand all they said, Joe, they squealed without a heavy touch!"

Joe began to be interested; he was very anxious to believe this, and to believe he could win Atkill's death ray. "Yuh—how ya know this Wilson bird ain't lyin'?"

"Joe, he wouldn't. He thought I was his best friend. He was spouting forth the confidences of his dried-up little heart.

"And he even told me all about the fence, and the other things they have there. Why I can give you a map of how to get in there now, and how to get out again. I'll give you a suitcase that's got a machine in it that will keep you from affecting their traps. You know how an old radio set squeals when you take the shielding off? Well, that's because your hand gets near it, and upsets the balance. That's what they are using, and all we have to do, is to put an electrical shield up, and they'll never know you're there.

"Get three men here, Joe, and I'll show them how to do it. I even know just where the papers I want are."

Joe was succumbing. That Death Ray sounded good, the thing sounded easy now.

"Yeah—but what about that fence? Mike said it kicked like a damn mute?"

"Certainly," replied Atkill. "Tell him to take a good hold on an electric light wire, and see how it feels. Just plain ordinary electricity. Everyone of you ought to know that."

"O.K. I ain't tellin' 'em, though. You give 'em orders, an' if they squeal, that's your bad luck," decided Joe.

An hour later Atkill was giving orders and demonstrations in his laboratory. He didn't mind. He knew that both Warren and Putney knew who it was that was ordering this attack on their papers. So he showed the men that his machine prevented their being detected, showed the film of gray-white paint on the suitcase that flamed greenish when ultraviolet light struck it, and gave them a map of the grounds.

Ten minutes later the three gunmen headed for the New Jersey Monorail.

CHAPTER SEVEN

THE laboratory was lit brilliantly by long gray-white glowing tubes filled with carbon dioxide gas. The glowing tubes gave a light precisely imitating that which streamed in through the great steel-framed windows, casting a pattern of trapezoids on the gray floor. But the gray-white tubes gave no shadows in this place where a shadow might mean an irreparable accident.

The tripod towers were finished, and the great silvery domes glowed under the clear light. There was no quartz tube connecting them now, only the three great magnets and two long rods of aluminum that failed to meet by a few inches, just between the poles of the mighty magnets.

Motors were humming softly, and a half-score of men stared up at the aluminum dome on the left.

"How's it going, Ran?" called Putney. His voice was steady, but inside himself he felt anything but steady. He had tried to argue with Warren, he knew that Warren should not risk his invaluable brain, that some man, whom the world might replace, should take that chance. That was reasonable. But it wasn't right, and he knew it in his heart when he tried to make Warren agree. Now Warren was in the aluminum dome, and no man on earth could reach him to argue more. He was protected by an enormous and rapidly increasing charge of electricity.

"Sixteen and a quarter million volts," called Warren exultantly, "and rising." Minutes went by and the steady hum of the motors continued, the soft slap-slap-slap of the silken ribbons that carried their charges up, and came down for some more.

"Seventeen million volts!" called Warren. "It'll be seventeen and a half soon. The leakage is almost nothing. Switches ready?"

"Right, Ran," replied Putney steadily.

"Make sure all the electroscopes, both recording and visual are charged, train your bolometers and other instruments. Check up, then for God's sake, get behind that lead screen, and use the periscope."

Swiftly the men checked over a bank of instruments all focused on the little spot of space between the three great magnets. Then they retired behind the heavy, curving sheet of thick lead that sat against one wall. A broad periscope mirror would send the light to them without sending the harmful radiations, for in its path it passed through a four-inch-thick plate of ultra-violet opaque glass.

Warren watched the instruments before him. The needle of the electro-static voltmeter device was quivering at 17+ now. His swift eyes swept the meters and saw they were all registering correctly. Then at last he stepped into a tiny lead closet built in the center of the aluminum dome. The entire interior was lined with heavy, thick milky glass, save one port of clear glass. There were various meters here, and two long glass rods.

His face was flushed as he saw the voltmeter reach the seventeen and a half mark.

He tripped the green-handled glass rod. There was a wrench, a tautening, and the meter jumped as the magnets went on, and the motors below whined to a stop.

"Here She Goes!" He pushed the second rod. There was a brief flare of light as a bit of iron wire suddenly exploded into brief incandescence, then a sudden terrific wrenching,

and a tremendous wave of smashed air as the awful power of seventeen and one-half million volts jumped across a six-inch gap.

Then a second wave came, a wave of flaring, infinitely bright, and almost palpable white energy, a cascade of light that beat down from a tiny point between the great magnets.

Matter was vanishing! Thrown into another space, it was rapidly disintegrating!

There was a sudden whine and screech as motors started, and the magnets lowered rapidly away from the glowing electrodes of the static generator. The point of blazing incandescence followed them and rested between their poles. The crane that supported the magnets swung them swiftly to a powerful machine on the floor. There was a thud as heavy plungers shot home, and a second snap as others shot free. The blazing ball pulsed larger for the briefest fraction of a second, and dived suddenly for the machine. It stopped, and hovered like the white flame of a torch over a small hollow in the top of the black cube of the squat bulk. It shrank, and burned steadily and clearly with a brilliant white light.

"Readings!" called Warren exultantly. "X-rays—none. Cosmics—none. Ultra-V's, none detectable. All radiation seems to be in the visible, principally in the blue-white range. When first started there was an instantaneous shot of cosmics and others, gamma, X and Ultra-V's, but they damped out instantly. You win, Ran, you win!" called Putney joyously.

Warren appeared suddenly, and slid down the quartz rod to the floor. In an instant he was running toward the squat machine, Putney behind him.

"How long can it last without additional fuel?" asked Putney as they ran.

"God knows, Putt. An hour at least, though. I can't tell how much the magnets captured and how much escaped when it went up in incandescence."

Warren cautiously moved a control. The brilliant ball seemed to expand, but the radiance died down, its color remained, but it was dimmer.

"Can't go lower, it's at the minimum now. Shall I try the fields?"

"Eventually, why not now?" replied Putney soberly.

Warren adjusted several rheostats, and read the meters carefully. Then he threw a heavy switch. The ball of luminescence quivered, and dulled to an orange color. A meter moved, and across the room a huge bar of rustless steel glowed red. Presently a second of the score or more glowed. The ball grew smaller, and under Warren's manipulation turned white once more.

"It works, Putt, it works," Warren almost whispered. In less than a minute the entire grill, of more than twenty heavy steel bars, was glowing bright red over its entire fifteen foot length. The laboratory was swimming in heat, but the men scarcely noticed it.

"Feed it!" urged Putney.

Warren cautiously turned a small button. The ball suddenly quivered and darted down slightly. A line of red, a fine steel wire had appeared in the center of the hollow bowl-like depression it swam upon, and the globe of embodied energy perched on it. The great bars suddenly glowed brighter, white hot, and began to slump swiftly. Only Warren's quick manipulation saved them. A faint hum from the globe of energy seemed the only sound in the room. There was a queer pulsing in the machine before them now.

"It works, Putney, it works all right. I couldn't somehow picture it happening. I could see that it should. I thought it would, but I didn't believe. That's it, Putt. Matter going forever, irrevocably." There was awe in the physicist's voice.

"The question is," Putney reminded him practically, "will it continue to go forever?"

"Let's start, then…"

That was two days before Atkill spoke to Wilson, and for the next three days the men worked constantly, observing, collecting data, then calculating the meaning of the things they saw and the things they were able to do. By the third day a tremendous amount of work had been done, and on the evening of that day the first fire, the Promethean Torch of atomic fires, had been transferred. Now it rested on a tremendous block of solid iron, and set about it were the dozens of instruments that controlled and directed its work. They had learned many things, and done many things.

And Putney was drawing up their patent claims now. Immediately after the fire had been started the men signed a joint statement in the presence of a Notary Public, and the document was post-marked. It proved the date of the discovery.

CHAPTER EIGHT

THE shadowy men moved cautiously forward over the rough ground. Their autogyro had descended with the engine off, and had made but the faintest rustle, and now they were cursing softly, as branches broke under their feet with the multiple snaps and cracks of light artillery. A city-bred crook in the woods at night is a forlorn creature.

Finally they reached the clearing, many bruises were on their shins, given by unseen rocks that sprang suddenly into a seemingly clear path.

"Any light in the green stuff?" asked Gorilla Mike.

"Nope. That light you can't see isn't on. Must be a hell of a light you can't see. What good does it do 'em anyway. Course those damn light-beam traps have some sense, but they don't floodlight the place," muttered Shorty.

They approached the fence cautiously, and no sign of the green flame came from their simple detector. Likewise the fence got no impulse from them as they came toward it. Presently Mike used a heavy pair of bolt clippers, and snipped several wires and rods of steel. He lifted the lock out of the gate bodily, and opened the way. They filed in cautiously, turned abruptly to the left, and followed the fence for nearly seventy-five feet. Then they cautiously set off across the grounds toward the laboratory building, bulking dim against the light gray of the clouds racing across the sky. A bright moon beyond threw a dim radiance on and past them. But they really had little to fear from any natural light, for as Atkill had learned from the too talkative Wilson, Warren was much more willing to trust to the abilities of his electrical and ultra-violet watchers than to those of any human watchers.

The suitcase, which had been humming softly, suddenly began clicking and humming in jumps and starts. Shorty looked down at it dubiously. Was the thing going wrong now, and leaving them marooned inside the fence? Suddenly he gave a cry of surprise, and pointed to the hitherto invisible streak of dirty-white paint. It was flaming with a blinding brilliance. Atkill had chosen his fluorescent paint well, and it reacted even to the long ultra-violets Warren was using.

With a curse the men turned to look for the light, to shoot it out. The scene was dark as before. No faintest glimmer lighted the scene. Shorty looked at the signal again and doubted. His eyes told him there was no light. This thing said there was. The suitcase was humming and clicking madly. The thing was broken. If there was light he could see it.

"Hey, are yuh goin' ta stay all night?" demanded Pete Constanti.

"Is this thing working or not? 'At's what I wauna know."

"He said yuh couldn't see the light. Let's get out."

"Beat it then," ordered Shorty. The three men turned and raced for the open gate, taking the shortest route. They hadn't gone ten paces before a blinding white beam of light caught them, and held them. Constanti pulled out a long-barreled revolver. He fired twice and the light went out. They ran on desperately now, and then a third spotlight fell on them.

It took time to shoot them out, and there were lights in the laboratory now. But they ran on again, and no more lights struck them. Presently the open gate stood just before them, wedged open by a piece of rock. Shorty dived for it, and as his body started to pass through the gate it seemed to strike something, a something like a very strong sheet of India rubber. There was nothing but empty space there, but Shorty bounced back heavily. He sat down even more heavily, and jumped up with a howl of pain, for there was an outcropping of bare, rough rock here.

The two following him hesitated in amazement, rushed hurriedly forward, and gave low cries of astonishment as their hands felt it. It was soft, yet almost as unyielding as a wall of steel padded with thick rubber. An inch it would yield, then it was immovably fixed. Pete Constanti had his long-barreled revolver out in an instant, and he sent three shots whining into the invisible barrier. Each gave a soft whine as it struck, and a second soft whine as it bounced from the barrier as from some marvelous spring. Luckily the bullets had not been aimed straight ahead, but at an angle and they did not return to their sender. They whined away to strike with a distant plop somewhere on a rocky outcrop.

"I wouldn't shoot," said a monstrous voice, "because the bullets will just bounce. Come to the laboratory."

The voice was very loud, and there was a slight mechanical timbre to it. But also there was a cold, deadly tone that made the three think of the tales two other men had brought back from this place of unknown horrors, of invisible walls that bullets merely bounced off, of invisible lights, and incredible and unknowable things that watched your every motion. Like trapped animals they hurled themselves at the barrier. Shorty Grimm hurled the suitcase with its load of batteries and mechanisms at the invisible wall, and it merely fell harmless.

"Come to the laboratory, immediately," the Voice said.

"Wat we gonna do?" quavered an affrighted Gorilla Mike. "You got us inta this, for God's sake get us out."

"We—we better go, I guess," Shorty said in a low voice.

Something pushed him from behind, something soft, but unyielding. With a cry of terror he ran forward, the wall was following them, pushing them. He ran, but not more than ten paces before he struck another of those invisible walls.

It was dark, horribly, weirdly dark, but the suitcase still flamed, and the lights of the laboratory glowed. All he knew was that before and behind were walls, walls that he could not see, and could not break through. Desperately he pounded on them, hurled himself against them. They did not even hurt him. He felt as though he was in some asylum, locked in a padded cell—a padded cell whose walls he could not see.

He began to laugh. Mike and Constanti looked at him with blank, fox-like faces. The laugh was very low at first, just a chuckle. Then more chuckles, then a wild, mad laugh that rang out. His pals could not understand.

Pete hit him and he fell to the ground. Mike looked on uncomprehending. Constanti bent over the fallen figure, and in a minute the man was stirring again.

" 'Tanks, Pete. God, it's like a padded cell, Pete. Let's go to dat lab-ra-tory. Maybe they'll let us out."

Anything seemed better than this. They started toward the laboratory, feeling for the wall, but the wall had moved. The Voice spoke again. "The walls move with you. You can move toward the laboratory, but in no other direction."

Presently they stood in the gray-white light that streamed from the laboratory door. Two great towers rose in the room of concrete, two half-dismounted things. They looked bare and ruined, like half-cleaned skeletons. In the center of the room was a great mass of iron, and around it nestled half a dozen mechanisms with long pointers of gleaming silver pointing at a glowing ball that floated unsupported just over the glowing top of the massive iron block. There was a slight depression under it, as though some acid had eaten at it slowly.

A half-score of men stood just within the doorway, looking out at them. Another man was seated beside one of the machines grouped about the central massive block, a tall, powerfully built man, with blond hair and gray eyes. His face was set and looked unpleasant. His fingers were working at controls before him. He looked up at them, and threw back a switch.

"Drop your arms," he ordered.

Half a dozen guns and three heavy knives came into view, to be followed by three slung-shots. Warren looked at them caustically.

"You're cheating," he smiled, but the smile wasn't pleasant.

"Honest—'at's all we got," objected Constanti.

Warren flipped a switch with another unpleasant smile. Constanti let out a howl of pain and snatched at something up his trouser leg, as suddenly Shorty Grimm howled and pulled a tiny automatic from his sleeve. He dropped it beside the knife Constanti had produced.

"Step back from the weapons," ordered Warren, and as they retreated, something shimmered for an instant in the light, and a curtain seemed to roll over the weapons. Warren threw over another switch, and a series of explosions like Chinese firecrackers rang out, then the smoke floated away, and there was a little pool of white-hot, sparkling metal on the smoking ground.

"All right, come in," he ordered. The three gangsters came because they couldn't do anything else.

"Who sent you?" demanded Warren sharply.

"Aw, we ferget," snarled Grimm.

"That's too bad. You like that padded cell you can't see? Or do you like this?" Something flashed around them resembling a sheet of water, and they were standing in the center of a hollow cylinder of milky light.

The light twisted and flowed in swirling currents.

"Touch it—touch it carefully," suggested Warren. "Better, stick your flask into it, and hold the neck with your handkerchief.

Constanti complied. He had whisky that was 85% alcohol in that flask. There was a faint crackling noise as the flask touched the beam, and the cylinder glowed faintly red for an instant, then relapsed to white.

"Enough—don't put your hand in. Drop that flask." Constanti stared at it instead. The flask was dripping moisture. It was white with frost, and drops of a light blue liquid fell from it in slow succession. He dropped it. The solid silver flask broke like glass, and the whisky within was a brown, hard substance that was coated with frost in an instant. It sizzled on the floor, and in a minute was melting and running away.

"Now—I think you have too much space. I'll close the column. If you want to talk—talk."

The milky cylinder began to contract, and as it grew smaller the men within it felt an awful cold come upon them. Their breath began to show, and their ears grew numb. Swiftly the cylinder became smaller, and rapidly it grew colder.

Presently Grimm saw something else above them. It was a great, deep-violet roof, and it seemed to be made up of streamers that fluttered slowly down. It descended, and touched his head. They weren't streamers, they were more of that padded force.

"Atkill—he sent us," wailed Grimm.

Instantly the cold was gone, the milky cylinder sprang back to its original size, and the violet streamers vanished.

"How did you pass the fence?" snapped Warren. A delicious warmth seemed to seep into the chilled men. It was easy to talk and be warm. Nothing could stop this man of unknown things.

"He gave us somethin' in a suitcase. You held it in your han' and the fence didn' spot you."

"Where is it?"

"Down on the grounds. I threw it at the wall, an' it just bounced off it."

"Wait." Warren turned to his instruments. Something fell to the floor with a soft thud behind them, and the men turned. The suitcase lay on it's side. "Wrecked," said Warren tersely. "Delicate electrostatic counterpoise, probably, eh Putt?"

"Probably," replied the black-eyed man beside Warren.

"Wat saw us?" asked Shorty.

"Your suitcase protected you against any one of our electro-static detectors, but it couldn't satisfy three at once, and when you were within range of the fence, and of two other detectors, it quit," replied Warren with a grin. "What were you after?"

Briefly Grimm told him. Warren looked at Putney, and then at Grimm. He wrote hastily on a sheet of note paper, signed it, and passed it to Putney. He too read, then signed. "Good idea," was all he said.

"Take this to Atkill with our compliments. Where is your plane?" said Warren, passing the sheet in a sealed envelope to Grimm.

Grimm told him. Then something gripped him, something like the soft, impenetrable wall, but different in that it held him like a monstrous hand. It lifted him, and he shot through the door, turned, and shot down the hill, over the fence, and an instant later was standing beside the plane. The force released him and was gone. A moment later the man, his nerves still quivering, saw Constanti flying through the air, to land gently twelve feet nearer a huge tree. Constanti stumbled, gave a low moan, and stood up. "Madre de Dios!" he groaned.

They watched something black hurtle through the air. It was headed exactly for the huge tree. A shrill scream of fear rang out as Gorilla Mike saw his end at hand. The force that carried him bore him toward the tree, and suddenly there was a crash, the great tree snapped over— and fell majestically away from the three men and the machine.

Gorilla Mike scrambled to his feet hysterically crying, unhurt. The forces were gone.

But it was an hour before their nerves quieted sufficiently to let one of them take the 'gyro aloft, and toward New York.

CHAPTER NINE

THE dull gray light of dawn was just creeping in through the windows. Atkill was sitting on the edge of his bed, and there was an expensive English cigarette between his lips. Shorty Grimm sat across the table from him. His face was white, his hands trembled and his breath reeked of cheap whisky. There was a bottle of Atkill's private and very fine stock on the table, and a half empty glass between it and an overflowing ash tray. Grimm's eyes held a look of blank horror and terror.

"Gawd, Atty, I saw it. I saw Mike flyin' through the air, then I saw him fly inta that tree—then the tree fell down, and there was Mike, cryin' like a baby, and laughin' somethin' awful. A man ain't meant to laugh that way.

"But that Thing seemed all soft, like a rubber sponge, but it knocked that tree down so easy but didn't even jar Mike. And that white thing—like a big cold ghost all around us, and we could see through it like a fog. It was so cold it froze Pete's whisky, and that's good strong stuff he gets."

Atkill laughed, a queer, little, strained laugh. "It was a lot colder than that, I suspect. Tell me, it turned white? But did it get wet, and—water—blue water drip from it?"

"Yeah," replied Shorty amazed, "how'd you know?"

"It wasn't water, it was air. I didn't know—I guessed."

"But—but air ain't like water. It ain't ever a liquid," objected the bewildered gangster.

"It is," replied Atkill patiently, "when it gets cold enough. You probably saw the coldest flask that ever existed. It probably didn't have any heat at all—absolute zero." He ruminated silently. Then stretched and stood up.

"Sorry, Shorty, but I guess you didn't get hurt. I really didn't think he would hurt you. He probably should have wiped you out, of course. I'll bet you anything he could have put you where they'd never find you within the next hundred million years," he smiled unpleasantly, and Grimm looked more unhealthy than ever. "He could probably have put you on the moon without trying, or hidden you in space.

"It's no use though now, Shorty. He's found the secret. You know that ball of white fire you saw on the iron block? That little ball of fire was giving off more power— could give more power than all the rest of the power plants on earth combined. That ball of fire could have stopped this planet, and made it turn around and go the other way. It could have lifted this whole city off the map, and put it down in the middle of the Pacific Ocean, just as easily as it lifted you and put you down in the middle of a field, or the middle of a tree for that matter. There's only one thing that could stop that little ball of fire," he went on, more to himself than to Grimm.

"'Wat's that?" asked the awed listener.

"Another one like it, only bigger, Shorty—another one like it." He smiled to himself.

"You failed—but here's a grand for your trouble and— unpleasant experiences." He handed a bill to the man, and waved him out. Nestor would pay the expenses.

He turned out the light, and went back to bed.

*　　*　　*

"Hello, Nestor. Got news for you," said Atkill as he came into the sedately luxurious office.

Nestor looked up eagerly, his shrewd eyes snapping. "What?"

"I sent some men to steal the data from the Putney place, you know. They came back last night, or rather this morning, and told a wild tale about being surrounded by walls they couldn't see, that pistol-bullets bounced off of like rubber balls, that let light through, but wouldn't let them out. Then they told me about a ghostly, white cylinder that nearly froze them, and about a ball of fire the size of a basketball resting on a block of iron. And they said something soft picked them up and hustled them out of the laboratory, and flew across the field with them. It set one of them down in the middle of a tree—after knocking down the tree without jarring the man.

"And he brought me this." Atkill extended the note Warren had sent.

"He's done it?" asked Nestor sharply.

"Obviously." Atkill returned contemptuously.

The note was as follows:

Messrs, Atkill and Nestor:

We feel it advisable to announce our success in our experiments to you first of all men. It will not be worthwhile to make further attempts to steal the data you are attempting to get. You will find full particulars in the patent specification and claims filed three days ago.

We don't like to make threats, but we wish to advise you that this laboratory is adequately protected.

Compliments to Atkill on his clever electrostatic counterbalance.

Randolph T. Warren.

Donald M. Putney.

Nestor snorted. Then he sat back sorrowfully. "It looks," he decided, "as though that ungrateful fool wins."

"He certainly isn't a fool," smiled Atkill. "And I don't think him particularly ungrateful. You had him fired so he'd be of more use to you.

"And I thank him for that compliment. It was a clever device. One of the cleverest dodges ever devised probably."

"Well, you may agree with him," Nestor retorted angrily," but at any rate you're through. Get out."

"One hundred thousand dollars first, please." Atkill replied smoothly.

"Huh? Why? You didn't do anything but cost money. You go read your contract, and you'll see that if you lose you get $100,000 minus the cost of apparatus, which was— let me see—seventy-five thousand so far." Nestor sat back with an expression such as that worn by a cat after the untimely demise of the canary.

Atkill looked at him coldly, very coldly, and a flame of murder, of equally cold murder, lurked in his eyes.

"Oh, is that it? Very clever." He paused, and the look in his eyes changed to rapid calculation.

"All right, will you let me leave *my* apparatus there in your laboratory until I have that twenty-five thousand in my bank?"

"Certainly," smirked Nestor. "I'll give you a check."

Twenty minutes later Atkill left with a check for twenty-five thousand dollars, which he had certified as soon as he reached the bank. He put it in his safety deposit box, and went on in the even tenor of his ways. He had Nestor's written agreement to leave the apparatus as it was till he had his twenty-five thousand in the bank. He also had Nestor's check, which could not be stopped, and proved nothing till he cashed it.

Atkill had received no money. And he would receive none till Nestor paid him the rest of his fee, in order that the bulky apparatus might be moved from a costly laboratory, which was now thoroughly useless.

Nestor on the other hand, felt that that unhappy business was well completed, so far as it touched Atkill. On the other hand, he was not through. He began doing some deep and serious thinking. Presently he called up William J. Fordham, President of the Atlantic Power Companies. He also arranged to have Arthur Benholt, of Central States Power and Thomas Ringman of Pacific Coast Power Lines on the wire.

"Gentlemen, this is Thaddeus Nestor speaking, and I have something of great importance to tell you. It is too important to trust to the wire. Let us all meet in St. Louis tomorrow noon. Is that satisfactory?"

"What is the basis of this important item?" asked Fordham cautiously.

"An invention, an invention that will wreck every power company, every air line, every railroad and steamship line, every industry in the world! I have been assured by competent men that it would ruin every power company within a week of its announcement. It must be stopped."

"We'll be there," said Fordham slowly. The others agreed, and began crossing off appointments on memo slips.

Nestor's assurances had weight.

CHAPTER TEN

"WE are all here now, Nestor. And all very anxious to hear what you have to say. What is this invention that can have such effects?" demanded Fordham. The big, gray-haired ruddy-faced man looked nervous, and worried.

"Atomic energy," said Nestor shortly. The three men started, and gasped slightly.

"Are you sure?" asked Ringman in a slightly unsteady voice.

"Atkill was working on it for me, and in the meantime Warren did the job. Three of my men brought back tales of some of the things he could do." Briefly he told them of Atkill's report, and the men's stories.

There was a long silence as the men thought of the meaning of this.

"Then—then he can put us out of business," said Benholt heavily.

"Without even a battle. He can sell mega-watt hours for what you sell watt hours. He can make airships that don't use engines, just tiny spots of that fire. We're ruined if that invention is sold. That is, if it is sold by him," he added with a sly look.

"Yes, if he sold it to some company—"

"But on the other hand," Nestor interrupted, "if he should unfortunately die, why perhaps his heirs would not display his acumen. He has no brother, nor sister, no near relative. I have investigated, and the only relative I have located is a second cousin once-removed. He is a teller in

147

a country bank, and his name is—James Oswell Jessop. Mr. Jessop has a wife and three children, he is about forty-five years of age, and I am sure, would consider fifty thousand an enormous fortune."

"If Pacific Coast Power Lines fail, I loose three hundred millions, and the other investors loose another billion and three quarters," said Ringman. His voice was shaky. The temptation was great—and he knew what Nestor meant.

"What could we do with the patent if we had it, that we could not do by buying it?" demanded Fordham.

"Cover it up," snapped Nestor.

"Why couldn't we do the same if we bought it?"

"Do you think for a second he'd let you? He'd sell you the power rights, yes, but he wouldn't sell you the other rights that it involves."

"Why not buy it and use it ourselves?" asked Benholt doubtfully.

"Because," said Nestor with a deadly quiet in his voice, "because there won't be any power companies after that is on the market. Don't you fools see that they won't need an outside plant for generating power? Don't you see that trains, factories, small towns, apartments, and perhaps homes even, will simply use an individual plant. Why is a big plant used today? Because it's near a waterfall, near a coal mine or near a number of big towns, and because a big plant is more efficient than a small one. And because they require skilled supervision.

"Atkill says this can be developed so that it will need no supervision. And it certainly needs no wisdom to see that no fuel is needed save a tiny bit of matter, iron evidently. Who cares for efficiency? Why worry?

"Warren won't sell power—he'll sell power plants!"

"Now, do you see why you can't let that invention become public."

"And where do you come in, Nestor?" asked Fordham softly.

"He'd ruin my aircraft business in an instant; he'd ruin every industry I have a touch in, except the iron and steel industry.

"And I couldn't buy him over before he completed his discovery."

Fordham smiled bleakly. "And what would you have done had you been able to get it?" he asked.

"Used it myself, naturally." replied Nestor. "And what would you have done in my position?" He looked shrewdly, and frankly at the bigger, younger man.

"Well, what are we going to do?" asked Ringman, raising his head from his hands.

"Wait. I think that we will know as soon as Warren gets his patents filed. At present he has only a half dozen sealed envelopes of Process Discovery. When he's completed his research and not before, he'll turn in his patents. In case we could discover anything, his filed patents would prevent our using it.

"On the other hand, if we wait, and he were—to die—why we could buy the completed patents from his heir, Jessop in this case."

"And what do you want of us?" demanded Fordham.

"Your help," replied Nestor. Then rapidly he outlined his plan to them.

*   *   *

"Lord, Putt, there are more things and more angles to this than a common housefly has eyes. We certainly wouldn't be able test all these things here on Earth. The explosive for instance—the disintegrating field. About half a dozen of these things can't possibly be tested here on Earth, and the only answer is—go into space and try it on an asteroid. We'll have to build a flying laboratory," said Warren.

"I agree—for more reasons than one. Now what sort of a thing had you in mind?"

"A dirigible-shaped ship, approximately two hundred feet long, and just about thirty-five feet in diameter. We would mount several big energy centers in the exact middle of the ship. We have found the gravity-field secret, and can use that to our advantage. The walls of the ship could be made of beryllium, perhaps eight inches thick for emergencies—"

"Beryllium—eight inches for emergencies," exclaimed Putney. "Lord, beryllium is so—I forget. It's impossible to buy, but we can make all we need. All we need is a sufficient amount of some other element! But then, eight inches for emergencies! That's no more than a good wall in space," protested Putney.

"Uh-huh—that's why it's an emergency fixture. We won't use material walls, we'll keep a permanent wall of force. The X-S73 field. Meteors—nothing will pass that."

"Right. Much better. And then how do we drive it?"

"Well, we could drive it ahead by simply moving the wall along. Since that is determined in space by the coordinates of our control, all we would have to do is advance them.

"However, why not use the gravity field as well? For high accelerations it would be a lot better. We couldn't use it here on Earth, or on any planet for that matter, but once free, we'd get a lot more acceleration, because we wouldn't feel it."*

"Good. Now those ideas—say I like this whole thing. We'll design that ship here and now, and Hultman can put the thing on paper for us."

They started then to plan the ship. *Prometheus* they called it, for it bore the torch of the everlasting fire that would light man's way henceforth.

THE gray concrete walls of the laboratory seemed bursting with the great lustrous thing that lay on the floor of the long, bare room. It was a shining, iridescent dirigible of metal, with long streaks of windows set in its side; curious projectors and little ports that seemed to open outward, studded the bow and stern.

But it was a beautiful thing, what one could see of it. The half-score of men who stood below and looked up at it now seemed mightily pleased with the great machine, over two hundred feet of shining, tapering metal. Across the bow, above the narrow streak of window, gleaming, golden letters a foot high stood out on the background of polished beryllium. "PROMETHEUS."

---

* The wall of force known as field X-S73 was created at any point the operator wished, by merely setting the controls. The coordinates so selected ruled the placing of the field in space. Thus by placing it at one point, and advancing the controls gradually, it simply moved through space, any force its movement applied, reacting directly on space, not on its source of energy. This apparent "lifting by the bootstraps" seems to defy the third law of motion, but actually the reaction is taken up by space, by the intertwined fields of a million millions suns. Similarly if the gravitational field was fixed in space, then the ship would fall into it, and changing its coordinates would move it along as did the force field.

"She works, Ran, she's magnificent." Putney's voice was low, and tense with excitement. "Around the Moon! In an hour we did what it took Sanderson six months to do! And old McCarthy finished those castings, and assembled her in three months!"

"It ain't a 'she,' it's a 'he'," grinned Warren. "Can't you read?"

"All right, heathen. The patents came through today," Putney added irrelevantly.

"There'll be more after we've finished experimenting. I think we'd better wait till we have everything, before we try to sell anything, don't you?"

"I agree, Ran. Well, we ought to find plenty."

"In the meantime—let's turn in. We can start tomorrow. The ship's stocked, ready, and waiting. One of you men want to volunteer for—"

The men started, and looked quickly toward a switchboard, half dismantled at one side of the room. A loud, humming note came from it, and a light blinked rapidly, more and more rapidly—and then there was a sudden terrific explosion. A huge crack appeared across one side of the room, the wall reeled, staggered, and collapsed with a terrific crash. Simultaneously the lights went out, and only a ghostly light came from a small flame, a clear white flame burning steadily on the top of a small block of iron, the size of a match box.

"Air raid—they're trying to kill us!" gasped Warren.

"Damn—into the ship!" roared Putney. The men leaped in at his heels. Putney whirled and raced down a long corridor toward the nose, up a flight of metal steps, two at a time, and flung himself into the control room. Flying fingers clicked over half a dozen tumblers, low thuds of closing plunger switches came from behind, and then a shimmering in the air about the ship, just as the second bomb flashed down. The great mass of concrete that was the west wall seemed tired. It began to lie down. Something seemed to stop it half a dozen feet from the wall of the ship, and it slid down on some invisible surface. A perfect rain of bombs pulverized it and every part of the building, before it completed its fall.

Something began to glow through the dust of the fallen building. It glowed white and clear, and seemed brightening rapidly. The dust had gone now, and a clear light shone over the scarred grounds, and the great ship shone like a heliograph. The light grew, and grew, the ground began to melt, the rocks commenced to glow bright as the awful flame increased in volume. A terrific roar of air grew louder and louder. Trees bent over, bent toward that spot where a draft of white-hot air was rushing up, the wind grew, and the trees toppled, rolled—and burst into terrific flaming gas.

"The little flare—the everlasting flame—it's broken free, and going faster!" somebody cried, from the rear of the ship.

"Putt—quick—we haven't tried it before, but we'll have to. X-785! Settings, take them: X-54-235, Y-87-452, X-32-81 and T-68 plus 436." Warren's voice rang out sharply, as he read from the notebook he had snapped out as he saw the flare growing. It was growing beyond bounds now—

Putney's flying fingers set the dials, then turned the little tumbler switch that threw the colossal power of the main burner into the field, a glowing ball of light ten feet in diameter, feeding on an eleven-ton ingot of iron.

There was a sigh, a soft, gentle sigh from all about them, and something wrenched at them, tore them apart, and hurled the separate individual atoms each in a different direction with an awful speed. The awful blaze of light was gone. The lights of the ship were gone—they were gone themselves, in an utter blankness.

*   *   *

SIX giant airplanes had come rumbling across the sky, their eighteen powerful gasoline turbines whispering softly to themselves, the fuel pumps chuckling gently, maliciously. Two pilots, one navigator, one bomber rode each plane, and with them went a huge cargo of high explosives, dressed in neat steel jackets. In all, there were thirty tons of highly explosive nitrogen compounds aboard the six planes.

They slipped through the air with scarcely a sound, specially silenced propellers, specially designed wings that merely rustled through the air even at two hundred and fifty miles an hour, and already nearly noiseless turbines. There was no sound, and practically no light. Only a faint glow from each plane, which was projected slightly upward. They could be seen only from above, and the leading plane was lowest. They were far from the lighted air routes here, and far from towns or houses, other than the dimly seen laboratory seven thousand feet below.

"Ready, Bert. Drop your first three," said the navigator of the leading plane. Three darkly shining ovals slid down through the starlight. They disappeared, then suddenly there was a tremendous flash of flame, and a roaring explosion a few seconds later. It was immediately followed by the detonation of the three bombs of the next ship, then the next, and the next. The buildings had opened out, and a great patch of light showed on the rocky hills. The second explosion darkened this suddenly, but in that instant, a gleam of metal had stood out in the lighted building, a great sheet of polished metal.

It was gone when the lights blinked out. Six heavy detonations, eighteen separate bombs, followed. Then silence as the planes turned for a second try.

Something began to glow down there. A fire had started perhaps? It grew swiftly brighter, a white, unwinking light that could not be a fire, it was too steady, too white and changeless, save for a rapid increase in brightness. The heaped ruins of the laboratory were already beginning to glow slightly, then brighter and brighter. They slumped, and a globe of white fire lit the landscape, and threw a brilliant stabbing light to the heavens that made the planes stand out brilliantly.

"Damn—searchlights—turn and drop everything you've got," ordered the leading pilot. Five other pilots heard his orders over their radio. The planes swooped, and turned. Twenty-four tons of explosives rained down toward the white light. They went off in the air as they approached, the terrific heat set the bombs glowing when they were fifty feet away, and exploded them instantly.

Suddenly the white died down, it flared brilliantly, blindingly violet-blue—the pilots screamed in agony, the entire planes turned red, and shooting flames sprang from the gas tanks. The turbines shrieked suddenly as though in agony, and burst with popping explosions.

Six flaming, white-hot planes dropped Earthward. They dropped toward a pit of white-hot rock half a mile across that heaved and boiled, and spewed forth great volumes of gas.

There was nothing else there. The ball of violet flame was gone, the laboratory was gone—and the six bombing planes were vanishing in blobs of white-hot gas.

The Putney and Warren Research Laboratories had vanished.

Next dawn a crowd of men were watching the still-glowing rock, and flights of airplanes wheeled slowly overhead. Newsplanes were taking pictures, telenews planes were projecting the view on ten thousand screens in New York and New Jersey. Beyond local interest, an explanation of the slight earth-tremor that had shaken the district, it had no meaning.

And a certain upstate bank cashier, one James Oswell Jessop, was visited by a lawyer from the firm of Powers and Mulroony, who informed him he was sole heir of Randolph Warren, who had unfortunately died in an accident in his laboratory the preceding evening. Mr. Warren was a scientist. Had he heard of him? Mr. Jessop had not. Had Dr. Warren left anything? Yes, a little something. A few patents. Would he like to sell them? Gladly—how much could he get?

Three weeks later he received the enormous sum of thirty thousand dollars for the patents that could have remade the world, blasted a thousand industries, and brought every nation of the earth trembling to submission before their owner!

CHAPTER ELEVEN

RANDOLPH WARREN raised a shaking hand to his head, and brushed back the hair that had fallen over his eyes. His mind was muddled, uncertain. There was a feeling of weirdness, of inexplicable things about him as he lay on the floor, even before he opened his eyes. The thick, soft carpeting of semi-sponge rubber was comfortable under him, and languorously he opened his eyes. He stared, raised a hand before his eyes, and stared harder.

His hand was a brilliant, flaming violet. His hair was a pale, virulent shade of green. He was wearing dark red shoes, dark orange trousers with twisting threads of a bright turkey red. His belt was pale violet. The gold buckle was slightly greenish in cast, but otherwise unchanged.

Lying on the floor nearby, and slightly stirring now was Putney. His lips were a dark violet, his hands the same bright violet that showed on Warren's own. His hair, normally brown, was now colored green, several shades darker, and much more pleasant in appearance than Warren's.

The physicist gasped, and sat up. The control room of his ship of course. But what had happened to it? It looked familiar, yet unfamiliar. The angles and proportions were wholly, utterly wrong.

And it was dark. The lights were giving a pale orange glow, but the window opened on a jet emptiness. Warren knew it was in open space, he could recognize that quality of empty blackness, but there was something very wrong with the sky, too. The very stars in their courses seemed vastly changed. He could not recognize a single familiar star, a single known constellation.

He heard a gasp of astonishment. Putney was staring at his hand with wide eyes. His eyes were bright, light blue, where they should be white, and very dark green where they had been black.

"You awake?" said Warren. "I felt the same way when I first saw my hand. Look at those beautiful red shoes you have on. How do you like my orange-and-red trousers?" His voice though, did not convey any sound of jocularity, but a feeling of helplessness.

"Where under the sun are we—what's happened?" gasped Putney.

"To the first I'd say, I doubt that we are, and to the second, I could guess, but I won't." The helpless tone of stupefied surprise was rapidly leaving Warren's voice, with a note of excitement following close on its heels.

Shouts and cries of amazement were coming from the rear of the ship.

"All men up here!" sang out Warren. Presently men began to file into the room. In a short time ten of the weirdest sights that ever met the human eye stood grouped before the two scientists. They were gaping at each other in speechless amazement. McLaurin, the burly Scots mechanician, was the prize specimen, however. He had on pale pink trousers, a light orange coat, blue shoes with red soles, and was now equipped with violet hair. A short time before it had been very red.

Warren burst out laughing at the sight of the dour Scot clad in this brilliant array of pastel tints. "Lord, Mac, was ever such a sight before?"

"An' o' course ye'r a beauty yerself," replied the Scotsman. "An' what may it mean?"

"Carl—you're somewhat of an astronomer, take a look out of the observation window. What stars do you recognize?"

"None—not a one!" gasped the young astrophysicist, after a keen survey of the star field.

"I'm afraid to turn the ship around right now, don't know what will happen, if my theory is right, anything might. Now where would you say the sun lay from here?"

Carl looked briefly out of the window that ran around three sides of the control room, and finally pointed straight astern. "Must be behind, we'd see it if it were anywhere else."

"Mac, run back and look."

The mechanist was gone scarcely thirty seconds before he came back, his face paled to a slightly lighter shade of violet.

"I can see through three other angles, Doctor Warren, but there is no sun!" he reported.

The men stared at him in horror. "No sun? My God, where are we?" demanded one.

"I can't say, but I can guess," replied Warren quickly. "This thing will get on your nerves if you let it, but take it easy. We are in a spaceship, the most powerful spaceship men ever knew. We are somewhere, obviously, that this spaceship, plus that little ball of fire, brought us. Therefore it's a reasonable conclusion that this same spaceship, plus an exactly similar ball of fire, which we can create, will take us back. Is it not?"

If Warren's theories were correct, it was not necessarily true, but the men nodded, hopefully.

"My theory is that we have gone where that matter went. Into another space! Not quite where that matter went, for remember we went through that, merely out of our own space, where there was no matter, and where no matter could exist. We exist, therefore we are in a space where matter can exist, but the conditions are different here, hence our violet faces, the weird coloring of our clothes and hair, and the feeling of unfamiliarity with this very ship we built. But the conditions are not so different that we cannot understand them, and live till we can control them.

"The first thing to do is to locate ourselves in this new space. We must take photographs. First, however, we must see that conditions permit our plates to work. This ship is completely stocked, luckily, so we have plenty of time to work. We must be in some part of this new space that corresponds with the solar system in ours.

"To get our position, remember that our own space is a curved hyper-sphere, a fourth dimensional sphere, roughly speaking, whose shape is maintained by the pull of the multitude of bodies, stars and worlds, which fill it. Now here are other stars—and probably other worlds. This, then, would be a space similar to ours, as one world is similar to another. Matter cannot exist between the two, but can exist in either, just as a man could not exist between Earth and Venus for instance, but, supposedly, could exist on either, but under different conditions of gravity, light, heat, atmosphere—everything.

"So it is, here.

"But one thing is not changed men, one of the most important things, I've still got an appetite, so let's eat!"

With a laugh of relief, they agreed with him on that, and started below. Two of the men set to work in the galley, preparing the meal, while Warren and Putney stayed in the control room, observing the meters.

"We've got gravity, we've got power, and light and heat, and evidently our force-screen is working, for there's atmospheric pressure outside, Earth-atmosphere brought with us. But what in—in the Universe did all of this?" demanded Putney.

"Conflicting force-fields, Putt, the conflicting fields of that little release-flame running wild, and our own field X-785. It threw us for a loss, Putt, but I think it killed that release flame.

"Now we've got to work fast, and locate ourselves. First and foremost, we'll have to use the telescope and take star-charts, so that we can come back to this point if we move, and by all the gods we will! I couldn't have done this in a billion years, and no man will ever do it again, in all probability, so let's make hay while the sun shines. Either we can return, or we can't, if we can, we don't have to worry, and if we can't, we might as well enjoy life while we live…"

"I guess you're right, Ran, but what will we have to do to learn about our position?"

"Determine the constants of space here. There are certain constants that are, I suspect, universal. The constant of gravity, the proportionality factor you know, will probably be the same, but we can determine that. But such fundamental constants as the velocity of light, radius of space curvature, the space equation of time and the resistance or rigidity of space constants, we will have to know. Evidently our release-flame burns steadily, though Mac said it was orange here—I'm not surprised—so we will have time to work. But most important for us, is the rate of progress of time as relative to our own space-time sphere."

"A second here may be a million years of Earth-time you mean?"

"Exactly—and if it is, we are forever isolated. By this time, or by the time we return, the sun and its attendant planets will have swung around the galaxy and been lost from us forever in a maze of five hundred thousand million suns, and the galaxy itself may have swung into some other part of our super-galaxy, the Magellanic cloud for instance—"

"Yes, and a much simpler way of being gloomy is to merely say we might all commit suicide. Let's go below," said Putney."

CHAPTER TWELVE

PUTNEY sat down gently in the comfortable chair in the "library" aboard the ship. It was also the conference room, study and den for the two friends. A phonograph was going in the after part of the ship now, and a good meal had put all in a better frame of mind. Warren sat down, after closing the door behind him. The glow of the tube-lights was steady and clear, the air in the ship warm and refreshing, and though the Earth was a countless inexpressible distance away in time and space, the warm air, the food, the music—all seemed to bring it near. Here in the heart of the ship, under the influence of the gravity fields, it seemed impossible that they were anywhere other than in their room on Earth.

Putney chuckled softly as he tamped down the tobacco in his pipe. "Seems scarcely possible, sitting here."

"Doesn't, does (puff-puff) it?" replied Warren, struggling to light his own pipe. "The question is, how are we going to get back, for we know it's not only possible, but a fact."

"Another question too, comes to my mind," said Putney softly. "When are going to get back?"

Warren looked at him sharply. Putney continued to look steadily at the ceiling. "Are we going to get back a few days after we left," he went on, "or are we going to come back a trillion years ago or a trillion years in our future?"

"As I before said...I don't know."

"Do you think the time-rates will be the same?"

"I know they aren't. The differences we see show the two spaces aren't the same. We can determine the time rate of this space in reference to itself—and I suspect it will be slightly different. What I mean is—we have brought yard sticks from our own space, but they have been distorted by this space. How much, we naturally can't tell. If we find by them that the speed of light is say 300,000 miles per second, by our also-carried-over clocks, then we know the time-rate here. But we can't determine the relative time-rates of the two spaces.

"Why? Would we be able to go back without knowing that?"

"I think we can, Putt. The power works here, evidently, and that time-rate change will affect all things equally, here."

"Suppose that one minute here represented an hour on Earth, and we spend a week investigating space-constants, then spend a year or so exploring. What happens?"

"Well—we'd get back to Earth a good many years after we started—sixty years late, wouldn't we, Putt?" Warren was thoughtful.

"So is it wise to spend any longer here than we have to? Seventeen years and our patents would be gone. By the way, what happens to them? They're made out in your name you know, and you are dead, and they can prove that you died in the terrible explosion of your laboratory. Some experiment we were working on went all wrong, and the laboratory was wrecked in a series of explosions. Probably fused into the bargain." Putney added.

"So that's what they'll say." Warren paused thoughtfully. "And somebody will inherit my patents, and then Nestor will buy them up, because the poor fool won't know what it's all about. I believe it's some distant cousin of mine who always made me want to take a picture of him. He's such a perfect model for the hen-pecked husband. Works in a little country bank."

"And the ten or twenty thousand dollars that Nestor will offer will be a tremendous fortune from the Gods, and he'll thank them on bended knees that they permitted you to live long enough to die and leave him something worth so much—when he could sell them for a hundred *billion* dollars. The nations of Earth would form a syndicate to buy those plans." Putney grinned sourly. "We were fools not to expect that."

"And Nestor and Atkill walk off with the gravy, don't they?"

"No," replied Putney, "they don't. I've been doing a little investigating, when Nestor started lying so very low, and being so very nice. Atkill got fired when he didn't beat you, and because he hadn't discovered it. Nestor had a win-or-loose contract with him, before Atkill took it, ten million if he won, and 100,000 win or loose. He lost—and got the hundred thousand. Only Nestor, the dear old fox, had a cute little apparatus clause. In case of loss, Atkill paid for the apparatus. It cost seventy-five thousand. Atkill was sore, and the two weren't on speaking terms— but American Super-power, the new Power Combine, and Nestor were surprisingly close. I was a bit surprised. Nestor told them the whole story, and said, quite truly, you could wreck them. They combined—and apparently bought a few bombing planes for good measure."

Warren's square-cut jaw was hardening. "You know," he said in a coldly precise voice, "I think we'll hurry right home—if we can.

"Let's turn in."

They started work the next day, setting up their apparatus for the determination of the all important space characteristics. They knew the exact procedure, and had trained men, and trained mechanicians, but the problem was not one of complex apparatus, but of many observations. They were enormously helped by the great power at their command, by the space fields they themselves could build, and by the mobility of their ship. But there was no star near them, and the nearest was more than two light-years away. It was impossible to visit it and get the assistance so much needed that only the enormous mass could render, but they did their best from a distance.

It was nearly two weeks later, by their chronometers, when the determinations alone had been made.

"And," said Warren, "that's only the preliminary. I've still got to find out how to use them. We've got to do some calculating. You know I took down the readings of all the instruments, don't you? As soon as I found what had happened, and where we were, I mean. And I had notes on that little laboratory release-flame, so I know the thing that threw us this way, and the character of that space, and I know the character of this space, so all I have to do is calculate what will do it the other way."

"Uh-huh. That's all," grinned Putney.

CHAPTER THIRTEEN

IN a city separated from the *Prometheus* by an interval that was inconceivable, and inexpressible in terms of Space and Time, was a shabby, dowdy building, in a shabby, dirty section of the city. Parts of the city were bright with streams of lighted cars and long rows of gleaming lights with moving walks and tri-level roads. Elevated trains hummed and roared across the city, and the soft light of stars and of a silvery moon were lost in the harsher, multi-colored glare of a giant city's lights.

There was a constant, husky whisper of city noise that seeped even so far into the dingy, dark section of the town, and into this room. A single, old-fashioned gas-glow tube lighted it. The woman who ran the boarding house was as frowsy as her house, and she had a poor sense of economy. There were actually some incandescent bulbs left, because they were cheaper—and 98% inefficient. The gas-glow tube in the room was nearly as bad, and the room was dim.

A scarred, tippy table stood in the middle of the room. A bottle and three glasses stood on the table, and beside them a large ash tray, half full. There were countless overlapping rings where "alcoholic" drinks intended for human consumption had made slight stains on the once-fine oak.

"Joe," said the black-haired man, leaning back in his chair, smoking an expensive briar, "I've got a job. This isn't merely a friendly call."

"Atty," replied Joe Keller, "I ain't sa dumb I dunno wen yuh'r here on business. Wat is it? Hope it's bettern the las' stunt yuh had." Keller was still a bit unhappy over the stories that had come back from the Putney-Warren laboratories, even though they had been three months old when the laboratory was blown up, and four months old now.

"It's a lot worse than that was, Joe."

Keller looked disgusted, pained, and unbelieving. "Hooey," he replied at length. "Even the D.T.s ain't as bad as that was. Hell, the guys wat came back here was all ravin' about it. I've seen 'em outa the D.T.s but they don' believe it after."

"Uh-huh—only this happened to 'em. They had reason to believe it."

"Suppose, Joe, yuh let this-here gentleman tell his yarn in his own partic'lar way?" suggested the lanky, bronzed individual with the sun-faded hair, on the third side of the table. He was handling his glass with an air of knowing what it was, and not believing it a substance to be downed rapidly in order to enter the state known as inebriation. His other hand was rolling a cigarette. It was a neat cylinder when he finished, and he inserted it into one corner of his mouth and lit it with what seemed one motion, and a puff.

"All right! Watcha got?"

"Texas, and you too, Joe, what would you say if I told you the United States was going to war? And it was going to war in about four weeks?"

"Huh?" demanded Keller. He sat up straighter. Even the lanky, easy-going Texan sat up a bit. "Who's got the idea they can swing *this* country?"

"Six men have. They're declaring war, or rather, announcing their rule. The first move will be complete destruction of all known fire-arms, the establishment of a secret police that has the power to execute on suspicion, and condemn without trial—and the removal of enemies."

"Hey—do you mean this?" asked Keller, his eyes narrowing sharply. He saw that Atkill was absolutely sincere. There was none of his air of laughing boredom now. He was deadly serious. He meant all he said. "I do. They intend to start with the United States, annex Canada, Mexico, and then take on European Nations."

"Who air these—here ambitious hombres?" demanded Texas.

"Old Man Nestor, and five associates, known as the Board of Control of the American Super-power," replied Atkill. "They own the patents that Warren worked out before the gentle souls bumped him off and bought them from his heir for thirty grand. They'd sell for one hundred million any day in any week, and a billion with no great difficulty. The poor fool was probably tickled to get the thirty thousand. And they get patents that will bring any nation on Earth to its knees…"

There was an unpleasant light in the lanky Texan's eyes, and his slight drawl had become much more pronounced. "And they feel that this here world is their private oyster, I reckon? How they figger they can do it?"

"They've got the Burt Hillen mob signed up for the job." Atkill's lips relapsed into a slight, grim smile. "And old Nestor is paying them half a million dollars a day. Then when they have finished getting control of the United States for him, Nestor figures they'll take their pay and get out."

Joe Keller whistled softly. "Sooo—tha's wat the Hillen mob's been up on. There's been strings out, sorta guesses, that they got sumpen big on. But who'd a gessed it was 'at big." He paused thoughtfully for several moments. "What are we gonna do, Atty?"

"What say we take over the ships they are building, and do the job ourselves," Atkill proposed.

The Texan looked at him sharply, then sank back a bit. Keller looked startled, thoughtful, and then finally shook his head. "No—we couldn't do it anyway, but—aw— somehow I like this ole U. S. A. I dunno—I wanna keep it. An' I'm damn sure I don' want Nestor and the rest of those big-wigs tryin' to run it. They'd—they'd wreck it."

"No," said Atkill with a hard little laugh, "they'd improve it immensely. Six strong men ruling the world with an iron hand—six strong men that could execute men on suspicion, without a 'fair, and reasonable trial' and without proving 'beyond reasonable doubts.' Trials that couldn't be beaten because somebody put a comma in the wrong place when the indictment was typed. Graft—hell, they'd make millions out of the country the first year. But six men would *rule* the place, and they would see to it they got all the graft that was grafted. And six men just simply can't graft as much as ten or twenty thousand that work at it now. Post offices where they were needed, not where they'd bring the most votes. No navy, no army, save those ten ships they're building now."

"Laws—half the laws on the books scratched off. Then perhaps two score sound laws that just couldn't be broken. When there's a police force that doesn't have to prove anything, then if that police force is honest and just, there can't be any great amount of crime. Mistakes, yes. They'd make 'em sometimes, but with all the courts, they make mistakes now. And it wouldn't be five and six years between crime and execution, either.

"On the whole, for the people that can't take care of themselves, it would be better. But they wouldn't like it, because they think they *can* take care of themselves. That's why card sharps and dips make a fat living.

"But I wouldn't want the country that way. I asked that question merely to see what you'd say."

"Waal—what we say don't make such a big difference, I reckon, but what we do, might. The question seems to be what air you aimin' to do about it?" asked Texas.

Atkill smiled. "Well, Joe, that sounds to me as though it was about to be business. You joining the deal?"

"Wat yuh think?"

"Well, let's make some plans. How's the gang, all the old boys with you—I mean other than Marty and Rabbit? They're taking a prolonged vacation I understand."

"Yeah—the State thought they oughta. It even proved they'd oughta. The rest o' the gang's ready."

"All right. Now listen, both of you." Atkill leaned forward tensely, and the others listened sharply as he unfolded his plan in that dingy little room, where history was being made that night, though none, not even the two listeners, knew it, only Atkill himself.

CHAPTER FOURTEEN

"You know, Putt," said Warren thoughtfully, "I've been wondering what disposition of the patents Nestor will make. We will be able to start the return process in a day or two, and I'd like to know what to expect. What have you in mind?"

"Nestor tied up with Super-power, as I told you," began Putney. "Now why, other than to get us out of the way? It would be easy enough to bomb us. He makes planes, and he no doubt knew who your heir was, and could buy the patents. Why did he tie up with the Power crowd?"

"That's your question. Maybe he wanted power, or perhaps he needed money."

"He'd need an all-fired lot before it got too big for him to swing. I think he could scrape up two million in cash, himself."

"How much did our ship cost, Putt?"

"Seven hundred and fifty thousand...three quarters of a million. It was a lot worse than I expected, too, because very few things were ready to hand. Even special furnaces had to be made after the beryllium was produced. It's lucky old Mac was ready for me, and willing to do it."

"He should have been," Warren grunted. "You saved his neck when Nestor was after him a while ago. What was the loan you made him—and he hasn't yet paid?"

"Oh, nothing much. He can keep the money as a darned good investment. I had a job paying him for the work on this ship. Anyway, I'm getting very fat interest."

"Well, the question is, Putt, what will Nestor and Power Incorporated do, and why did they wait three months after we discovered it, to bomb us?"

"They waited, to make sure there would be a copy of the plans somewhere, where it wouldn't be destroyed when we were, and they bought them merely as a formality, I suspect," answered Putney seriously.

"Huh? That's no formality—that gives them exclusive rights—"

"Do you think they're appealing to the law? No, not by a long shot. I'll bet that jolly crowd is making law by now, if time is faster there than here, and we suspect it is. Why did Nestor join? Because ships cost about a million apiece, and he wanted several ships. He knows plenty of gun-gangs that will throw in with him on this proposition. Listen, Man. Don't you realize that with this ship we could bring the whole world to its knees, take every dollar, every pound and every mark we wanted? Do you think any navy or air force could stop this ship for even thirty seconds? Do you think Nestor doesn't know that? He wanted the power-men in, because it made it easier. I'll bet they were willing enough too, when they realized just how valuable their power franchises would be with this invention on the market. Look here, Nestor wanted money. He wanted big money quickly, from someone of whom he could get a hold on, and the power utilities offered him an excellent chance. When they were accessories to the bombing, and supposed murder of our men, they'd hold together.

"They build the ships, from the patent diagrams they can get hold of easily enough. They are all ready to attack—and simply cut off all power over the United States. They destroy the plants, so that power can't be restored, except by the ships, for no other means are available—the nation without power—the railroads dragging out old steam locomotives that have been used for switching for the last two decades, and that are unable to move faster than a crawl. New York cannot get food in the vast quantities it needs it. Planes can't bring it. Ships can't bring enough, when all the distributive systems are tied up. No lights. No elevators—the whole city paralyzed for want of power, and in a state of semi-panic.

Then the ships. Unheard of—tremendously, deadly. Why, they could freeze the Hudson and the North River, and even ocean ships couldn't get there for days. Floods because of ice-jammed rivers. Do you see what would happen? They don't have to take the patents by due process of law—they just grab them, and then make the laws!"

Warren whistled softly. "Nice people. Wonder if they'll do that?" he asked speculatively to himself.

"Do it—of course they'll do it!"

"Will they be able to—I wonder what their men will say. They'll have to use gangsters, or train crews of equally unscrupulous men. Now having the country in their power, will they be willing to turn it over to Nestor and his crowd?"

"Nestor hasn't the conscience of a gangster, but he has a lot more brains. He's probably arranged some beautiful system for killing off everyone of his men, save one crew, of one ship, which he can absolutely trust. If I were doing it, I'd have a poisonous gas flask ready to release when a certain radio signal was given from the flagship. That would eliminate most of his problems. A secret police with full powers of execution without trial, would speedily eliminate all others."

"Ummm. Nice people, as I believe I have said." Warren's mouth twisted as though he had tasted something nauseous.

"What are we going to do?" he went on.

"We've tried out all those things you wanted to, at the expense of a few of our seemingly endless supplies of steel ingots. How many did you store by the way?"

"One hundred and fifty, Putt. There are one hundred and forty-one left."

"We'll simply have to go back and use them. Perhaps we can dissuade the Nestor and Powers crowd. We might wait till Nestor has removed his extraneous crews."

"How do you know he will, Putt?"

"Lord, Ran, he's no fool, and you stated the problem exactly. The gangs have to wait till he shows them how to win, he has to wait till they've won—and we have to wait till they've been cut down to our size." Putney said.

"—and half the population has been killed off?" continued Warren.

"Wait till we know what month it is when we finally get back," suggested Putney more practically.

*   *   *

A tiny sliver of moon floated rather low over the horizon. It was dark, very dark, and the stars seemed to cast no light at all. A tremendous shed loomed up against the starlight a short distance ahead, as the three large autogyros sank soundlessly to earth in the broad field. There was one square of light in the near corner of the great hangar, and across it fine lines seemed drawn. A wire fence stood between the newly-landed machines and the building.

Fully a score of figures tumbled from the three machines, and on the back of each was a peculiar pack that hummed very slightly as they advanced. Each man walked softly, looking occasionally at the leather strap about his wrist, carrying a small disc of some gray-white material. And each man carried a machine-rifle, a gun weighing little more than twenty pounds, shooting extremely high velocity .22 caliber bullets, at the rate of 300 a minute. The stock was thick, and carried a broad chest-plate to protect the firer.

Two low humming notes sounded softly, and the various groups of men moved toward the wire fence. One man, evidently the leader, carried a suitcase, and wore a peculiar mask over his face. In the other hand was a square, box-like apparatus which he pointed in many directions as he walked. Yet another man was leading him.

"Take it easy, Tex. I can see the fence all right, but this damned infra-red rectifier is blurry. It's not as fast as ordinary light you know, in the cells. There are four sentries walking about pussy-foot, and three more lying down. They haven't seen us, but they shine like blinding lights in this thing. They're sure radiating heat. More to the left."

The men went off toward the left. After a moment the masked man halted them, and sent forward two with heavy clippers. "Take it easy now," he whispered, "they've got electro-static charges on that fence, and you have to give your equalizer a break on that. Approach slowly, cut quickly, but don't make a sound. Hold the wires with your hands. Shorty, and you, Pete, cut gently. Go."

The two forms went forward, and disappeared from the sight of the others in an instant. Clouds had come up, and even the minute light of the moon was gone. Approaching with the hills behind them, they were invisible to the watchers beyond the fence, but the man with the mask saw them clearly as they cut a section from the fence. One man ran a wire about the section they intended to cut free, maintaining the circuit of metal, after the metal fence had been carried away, and finally laid gently on the soft turf.

"All right. Forward. Follow me," ordered Atkill, his voice muffled by the mask.

They went forward quietly. Twice Atkill turned sharply from his path as the mask spotted ultra-violet beam traps that gave off infra-red as well, despite the fact that no visible light escaped. Again he turned aside for a complex, electrostatic trap.

Finally the twenty-three men were less than thirty feet from the door, the door that opened into the office of the great hangar, and the only one not locked.

Atkill took off his mask, deposited the suitcase and the black box of the detector and cells on the ground, then took a Very pistol from Texas, and a machine rifle from Joe.

He pointed the Very pistol upwards, pressed it, and an instant later the rocket light flamed upwards. Two seconds later a far greater rocket soared, up from the planes, out beyond the fence, and an instant later a blindingly bright magnesium flare was drifting down from a parachute. The entire grounds were thrown into brilliant relief of clear, white light.

Seven men had turned at the sight of the Very light. They whirled, bewildered, at the hiss of the rocket beyond the fence, and stood rooted and blinded under the light of the magnesium flare. Twenty-three men had been standing by the wall, staring steadily at the lens of a brilliant flashlight, and their eyes were accustomed to the glare of light now. The machine-rifles spit viciously, and seven armed guards sprawled on the turf.

Simultaneously a howl of surprise and rage came from behind the door, and a giant of a man stumbled out to see the trouble. He sprawled dead before the pistol in his hand could speak, and three men charged over his body, shooting, into the guard-office. There were the heavier barks of automatics mingled with the snappish clatter of the small-caliber, high-velocity machine guns.

Three more men charged in behind them, ready to shoot. There was no need. Electric floodlights had snapped on outside now, and a siren was howling disconsolately somewhere, half drowning the cries and bellows of men. There was a rush of feet beyond the inner door of the office, men running across the concrete floor of the hangar.

The inner door went down with a crash as two men hurled themselves against it, through it, and began shooting inside. An echoing volley of heavy shots returned the lighter barks of the machine-rifles. Then came the heavy, rapid fire of a high-power non-portable machine gun. There were ten men inside the hangar now—and none of them had been wounded! They stood up under the blaze of light, and returned the fire of the enemy hotly, turning to face them rather than swinging their guns.

Suddenly one went down, the barrel of his gun a twisted mass of iron, the breech burst wide. His own gun had exploded as an enemy bullet struck it.

In twenty seconds there were no more shots heard inside the hangar.

"Ten men on the doors. Have your guns placed. See if the heavy machines here are workable. Defend the place as long as possible. They'll have the field guns working.

Chatter a machine gun to make 'em think they've got friends still alive in here." Atkill was barking orders sharply. Men hastened to do as he told them.

"Tex, Joe, Shorty and Pete—come." They raced toward a great dirigible-shaped hull of silver metal. The hull was completely formed, but there were ladders, mechanics tools, scaffolding about it. The windows were not all installed, the thing was not yet completed. "This'll do. It's the most nearly completed, come on."

Into the ship they plunged, ready with guns for resistance, but the mechanics had fled. Atkill found his way quickly to the power room.

Banked machinery formed a circle about a great block of rough, rusted iron. Dully gleaming control boards, with banks of instruments showed on one side of the great room at the heart of the steel-walled ship. The lights the men carried swept about.

"Tex, take off your pack." Texas seemed leisurely in his movements, but in a surprisingly short time the pack was at Atkill's feet. Atkill opened it quickly, and within it were tiny mechanisms like these giant machines here, a tiny control board, and a speck of iron, a blue-white flame of unwavering intensity burning above it. And beside it were two heavy copper bars.

Atkill rose, and looked at the mechanisms with apparent negligence, but with a glance that took in everything.

"Thank the Lord 'Boozey' wasn't too drunk to talk straight. She's ready to start. We'll need five and a half minutes. Joe, send every man out—they've started attacking—send every man out to the doors. Make sure they don't get in. If a shell blows a hole in the wall, put the men under the hulls of the ships. These walls are three feet thick, and will shed anything man ever sent—except fortes, and I don't believe they're using them. Go to it."

Instantly he turned himself, and with amazing precision adjusted a hundred complex instruments; he took from one of the packs the men had carried, three heavy copper bus bars, and in a moment had them connected with Texas' pack. These he connected to similar connectors on the ship's machines.

He was busy again with the dials. Finally he bent over the little pack, and turned something. The blue-white flame dulled, turned an angry red, and a low, powerful hum set up. Something seemed twisting, dragging everything, every atom of them, toward the massive block of iron, yet nothing moved them, they stayed where they were. There was a queer activity on the surface of the iron, and Atkill's black eyes stared at it sharply. The surface writhed, the rust seemed to dissolve, and powdered metal remained. Something seemed whirling just above the surface of the iron, the metal licked upward, and a blaze of sudden white light smote down at the men. The surface of the iron was white hot, and an instant later the burst of light came and went again, again and again, faster, then they merged to one, and a dull roaring set up. The ban of flame was a foot in diameter, growing swiftly. Atkill sprang to the controls, and made rapid adjustments, watching the growing, pulsing flame.

Something screamed outside, then there was a terrific detonation. A man cried out in agony, and running feet echoed across the concrete floor.

"Tex—call 'em in. We're going. We can't wait," ordered Atkill.

The Texan disappeared, shouted something. A moment later the lights in the ship flashed on as Atkill pulled a switch. They glowed, flickered, then burned steadily white. The tiny pack release-flame was glowing blue-white once more. Atkill stooped, adjusted something, and it shrank slightly. The great release flame burning on the block of iron was glowing steadily now. Scrambling feet echoed on iron. Texas stuck his head in through the doorway.

"Thar in."

Atkill pulled a switch, the release-flame dulled momentarily, and the crack and clatter of falling, severed scaffolding echoed into the ship. Something whined again and exploded heavily. There was a terrific crash as a portion of the wall fell in. The ship though, was undamaged. The force-field was up.

With a swoop of power, a crushing weight fell on the men aboard. Atkill looked from his window, and saw the walls of the hangar drop swiftly downward, then the slope of the roof appeared. With a terrific crash the ship smashed her way out through a hole torn in the roof, and vanished into the night.

Atkill smiled happily at the lank, tanned Texan.

"Did it."

Below, men milled about in the hangar, helping men caught under the fallen roof, attending to the wounded, who were few, and the dead, who were numerous, and their own, and calling frantically on a telephone line that didn't work.

An autogyro roared, and sailed away. A crowd of men swarmed from the hangar in time to see it disappear into the night.

Ten minutes later a second had been filled with gas, a smashed carburetor replaced, and the machine headed for New York as it took the air.

Burt Hillen was cursing furiously as he surveyed the wreckage. "The blankety blank son of a so-an-so. An' wat the hell happened to you guys? Yellah? My gawd the way yuh all lit out wen they showed up! Tha's the Keller mob, an' we're due to get that so-and-so. Go on—clean this joint up. They got one o' them things, an' I dunno who was wid 'em, but he got it started. That means we gotta fight THAT when we start—an' it's ol' Fox-face's private ship." He expressed his opinions at length, and stared at the hole in the roof through which the vanished ship had gone.

But it didn't bring back the ship, and it didn't bring back Atkill.

CHAPTER FIFTEEN

THADDEUS Nestor sat at the head of the table. The table was beautiful dark mahogany, the walls were hung with thick velvet drapes—and soundproofing materials.

Down the sides of the table the five other men, who represented the directorate of the American Superpower, were sitting, and listening to him anxiously, for what he had to say meant a great deal to them.

"And so, gentlemen, due to the inefficiency of our guards, the thieves stole that ship, the flagship. There are nine remaining ships, but none were quite so powerful as it. That, and the fact that it was most nearly completed, was the reason it was chosen no doubt, I doubt if they knew of—the arrangement as we may say.

"But I know who it was! It was that lying, murderous, crooked, untrustworthy blaggard, Atkill, with his villainous gang of cut-throats and murderers. I've seen to it that all our guards were notified of those who committed the theft and the attack, and I've taken the liberty to offer a reward of a quarter of a million for their capture, and the return of the ship.

"However, I fear it is useless. This blaggard is cunning, with the low cunning of rats. He forced me to pay him fifty thousand dollars for some junk apparatus I had foolishly given him permission to leave in my laboratory— the ingrate. I paid him one hundred thousand dollars for a month's work—and that's his return." Nestor truly convinced himself he had been badly handled. Now he was afraid.

"He has of course, examined those patents, and knows all that we know about the possibilities of the thing, but there is one thing that worries me. Warren mentioned artificial gravity in the presence of a certain man who has reported to me, a laboratory secretary named Wilson, and we have not found any means of producing artificial gravity.

"It is evident that there are more possibilities our men have not found. They tell me they understand it, but I'm not sure."

William Fordham, President of the Atlantic Power Corporation, Vice-President of the American Super-Power, interrupted. "They don't know what it's all about. They merely follow the directions of the patents, and they get a machine that does this or that, as the papers say. The fools can't even find out what makes it happen."

"Uh...I wasn't sure if they could," went on Nestor. "But Atkill's a brainy rat. I'm sure he has figured it out, and he may have something new that we don't know about.

"Now I wonder if it wouldn't be advisable to buy him and his group in with us. He could cause a great deal of trouble, particularly if he waited till after we had—er—discharged our allies."

"I vote we do," said Fordham.

The others concurred. "We'll buy him in then, at the lowest price we can," decided Nestor.

*   *   *

Burt Hillen was also holding a council that morning, and on the same subject—the manner of dealing with Joe Keller and Company. Burt was listening to an impassioned oration from "Tiny" Morgan. Tiny was six feet six tall, and four feet broad, and weighed 257 pounds. Also he could shoot so rapidly and so accurately that as long he was living a long time in gangland, he was much feared. Tiny's only trouble was one he did not realize. He had the bulk and strength of an elephant, but the brain of an ant.

"All yuh say may be perf'cly true, Tiny, but I heard of a yarn: about a guy wat wanted to make rabbit pie, and the first ting they said was to git the rabbit. Them gumps has got the ship, and they've gone. Try an' fin' 'em."

Somebody knocked on the outer door of the guard office. The pounding hammers on the ships and the racket of repairs to the great roof of the hangar almost drowned the sounds, but the signal knocks were recognizable. Burt reached out a hand and pressed a button. The door opened of itself. "Yeah?" he demanded. "Dumb" Bell, who served in the role of a secretary to the Chief of the organization stuck his head in. It was a wizened, bald head. The man looked about fifty, and was actually thirty-two. The face was sharp, and pinched. Aloysius Bell he had started out in life, but the name "Dumb" quickly attached itself, because he was markedly other than dumb, and because it suited his last name so perfectly.

"Chemmy's outside. Got sumpin' important."

"Huh? Chemmy? Oh, yeah. I had him come down didn't I? Sen' him in," ordered Hillen indifferently.

"Chemmy" was the chief chemist of Hillen's industries. He was foreman over the workers who synthesized the drugs the Hillen mob sold, and the alcohol they made into drinks. At one time he had been James Ogden Brent,

Ph.D., and a number of other things. He had, however, synthesized a new drug, tried it on animals, and found it harmless. He tried it on himself, and found it was so powerfully a habit-former that a single dose put him forever in its grip.

He was in the hands of the gang now, and Hillen had sent him out to look at the ships. Somewhere in Hillen's clever, twisted mind there lurked the idea that a scientist of his own should look over these scientific marvels, and pronounce them fit for him.

Brent came in, a little stooped man, his eyes unnaturally bright, unnaturally quick. "Hello. Hillen. Who built these ships?" he asked as soon as he passed the threshold.

"Huh? Old Fox-face's mechanics a course."

"Well, listen, if you go aboard those ships after the windows are in, he can kill you any time he wants, without touching the ship," snapped the little man.

Hillen stiffened. Tiny Morgan let out a bull roar of anger. "Yuh mean that?" asked Hillen softly, as he settled back. "How?"

"I was looking over the arrangements for the purification of the air in the ship, and I saw that the apparatus was cleverly designed. It will do its job very well. But there was one pipeline I could not understand, that led into the main return pipes—the pipes that would distribute the air through the ship. I also noticed something that I thought was a radio set, and as I could see no reason for a radio set there, I sent for 'Sparks' Cohen. He's the head of the communications department, and a very clever radio man. He told me that a certain kind of radio signal would, at any time, cause the value to open, and any gas that was in that pipe line would be distributed throughout the ship. While I was waiting for Cohen to arrive, I followed the pipeline back, and finally found a water tank that didn't hold water, but 'akalite'. Akalite is liquid, and it looks like water in the gauge, but actually it's a low-boiling liquid, so deadly that it will kill a human being diluted one part in a million in the air. The radio set could release that gas into the ventilating system of the ship, and kill the entire crew of the ship in less than ten seconds.

"Eight of the ships are so equipped; the ninth had been equipped that way, too, but all of the equipment has been taken out, all except the actual deadly akalite, which could only be removed with the aid of professional gas masks. That would have been noticed. As it is, the ninth ship is perfectly safe. It's the flagship."

"The one old Fox-face and his friends will ride on, isn't it? Beautiful scheme—bee-ut-ie-ful." A slow, hard smile spread across Hillen's face. "Verry, verrry pretty. So we takes the country fer him, and den he wipes us out—an' he has the whole works—and we have a swell funeral. Verry clever." Hillen's smile was cold, deadly.

"That—damn stinkin' double-crossin' Fox-faced monkey! The so-and-so wan'ed us to get in—an' den he wipes us!" Tiny was roaring again.

"Tiny," said Hillen coldly, "sit down."

Tiny sat. "Well, watcha gonna do—let him go? Hey, lemme get dat guy, will ya?" he demanded.

"Yes, Tiny, I think we let him go. Uh-huh. We let him go. We make sure he don't know we know. Then he'll go ahead; an' let us take the country fer him—only we'll be doin' it fer ourselves, see?" Hillen's face was smiling pleasantly now, he looked quite pleased. His eyes were black, and little gleams of murder dwelt in them. "An' after we've done it—when he's all ready, an' sends that signal, an' tries to turn on the gas—we'll turn somethin' on him, maybe…"

"Chemmy, call Sparks in here and we'll have a talk. Come on," ordered Hillen. His lips still smiled, and his eyes were beginning to smile when the chemist returned with the radio man.

CHAPTER SIXTEEN

"S-O-S—S-O-S—" On the air over the whole nation the dread letters came through. Radio stations shut down abruptly, every broadcasting station cut off the air, and twenty million television sets went blank after the brief announcement.

Strangely, after the letters came through, there was no message to follow, and even more strangely, the call was heard on every broadcasting wavelength!

Perhaps station attendants wondered at that, but they did not wonder long, for the strong, clear signals suddenly stopped.

"The air is clear. The message of the Council of Five will be delivered." A deep, powerful voice spoke, but no television disc signals came, no view of the man. Every wavelength gave the signals clearly. Everyone of the still waiting radio sets resounded with the deep voice.

"The Council of Five declares the United States no longer a republic. The Council of Five shall hereafter rule this nation, and within the year, the nations of Earth.

"The warships of the Council of Five will appear over New York City at ten o'clock tomorrow. Part of the fleet will appear over Washington at the same time. The financial and political capitals will be expected to signify their acceptance of the Council by the lowering of the conventional flag, and the raising of a flag whose field is bright blue, and on which appear five white stars, one in each corner and one in the center.

"Resistance is not advisable. The Council of Five has weapons beyond any known to the rest of mankind.

"The Council has spoken."

The air was silent. Perhaps many that night turned off their radios as they heard some part of an impossible play coming over the air, heard some lines from an author's flight of fancy.

But they began to believe soon, when they heard the cries of amazement and anger in a thousand towns and a hundred thousand villages.

Police and Army and Navy officials were busy now, intercommunicating, attempting to locate the center of the disturbance, whence that message came. It was hopeless. Their results were impossible. Apparently the message had started somewhere over Florida, and its sender had moved during the course of the message, till it ended over southwestern Washington. The thing was impossible. They gave it up in disgust, and perhaps in fear, and began sending orders. Troops began to move toward New York and Washington that night. Battleships started suddenly in the same directions. The Pacific fleet hurried toward San Francisco and Santa Monica, Seattle, and the other great west-coast cities.

Air forces moved swiftly, and before dawn a tremendous fleet of planes was congregated about the fields of Washington, D. C., and New York.

And high above both cities a dozen or so of the newest planes, the radio-guided and radio-powered ships swung back and forth. Noiseless—invisible in the blue—

Restless mobs howled and cursed sleepless all night, the troops fell to disciplining them as they arrived, and the lights of the city blazed till dawn. At dawn, New York and Washington time, every light went out, every train stopped, every line of transportation was suddenly dead. In both cities the power was gone, and across the whole nation the electric power ceased to be. Trains stopped, subways suddenly were motionless.

Chaos in an hour. The mobs went mad; struggling people in the subways shrieked and howled and roared as their disposition might be. But at the end of an hour trains began to move cautiously, only sufficient to get the people from them safely, elevators that had left men and women trapped one hundred, or perhaps more stories above the ground, began to work to carry them down, never up.

The city was drawing on its giant batteries. The power batteries that were intended for emergency came into use. There were no men in the power plants, and no power came from other cities, from outside. Army engineers threw in the batteries, then as battleships steamed into the harbor, great cables from their dynamos carried a measure of power across to the paralyzed city.

Telephones had operated, for they were maintained by the emergency power generators, which every station contains. Radio had failed, save the army portable apparatus, for the great stations depended on the power lines.

The Council of Five had stricken the city, turned a howling, angry mob of vengeful men into a paralyzed, panicky crowd, struggling to escape something they did not know what, that had completely disorganized their city, left them trapped in burrows under the streets, or in perches high above them. Here and there fires and terrific explosions had broken out, for the radio controlled and powered planes had come down, uncontrolled and unpowered, when the power failed.

Further, power would not be restored, the meager output of three battleships could not sustain the city, the tremendous batteries were not to be wasted. And the power plants were hopelessly wrecked. A small plant had gone first, destroyed by a sudden reversal of its phase, and it was pumping power against the power-tide of a nation. From transformer to generators all were wrecked. A neighboring power plant suddenly got the double strain—it went the way of its predecessor. Like giant snowballs ever gaining volume, plant after plant went, till finally half a dozen of the greatest alone remained, and the power load of the United States was thrown on them suddenly.

It would be months before effective power was available. Army engineers were rushing about in wild anxiety. There were guns, there were planes, but the thing they had greatest hope for had been the great, sleek tubes that had been mounted in a dozen places about the city. Fifteen feet long, their thick, glassy walls glowed red as the rising sun painted them. Inside the outer tube, an inner tube of copper reached up ten feet of the length, to end in a crystal glass tube. Great power-elements inside the glass, and a huge bowl of copper screening just below this juncture point told its purpose. These Harrell tubes were new, tremendous tubes that were simply radio tubes and sending sets in one combination, but they could handle a hundred thousand horsepower, and all that power was reflected from that curiously light, and ineffective-seeming copper screening, and it went out as a beam that was absolutely deadly to any man or animal and destructive to any piece of metal in its path.

But—to send one hundred thousand horsepower of radio energy, two hundred and fifteen thousand horsepower of electrical energy was needed. The three ships in the harbor could not quite supply the energy for one of these tubes—they had planned to use a dozen. The batteries would supply them and run them for ten minutes, perhaps. And if those flying ships the Council of Five had spoken of could move as they seemed to have moved last evening, no shell would ever catch them, only these beams, traveling at the Ultimate Speed, the speed of light.

Commander Gilbert C. Coache gave his orders very energetically, and very hopelessly. Secretly, he felt sure that the losses would be heavy. Guns could not cope with any ship that could display that speed—some rocket ship of undreamed of power.

He was very angry, and very nervous. He had been working now since the previous morning, and working desperately since the previous evening, when he had been given the command of the defenses of New York City.

"Power—power—damn it, that's all I want, Major. I can't do a thing if you can't give me power."

"I'm sorry sir, but the only form of electric power in the city are the indispensable telephone generators, three-quarter-full batteries, and the power from the ships. Boston, Philadelphia, Albany, Newark, why every city about has batteries that would give us all the power we need, but Lord, the damn things won't pump power through a transformer, and these lines are all A. C. lines. I'm as anxious as you—but I can't do anything. There've been at least six thousand nuts pestering me with bright ideas since I came here. One man wanted us to commandeer all the automobile batteries, and use them. But—"

"I SAID *power!*" Commander Coache hung up. He lit a cigarette, took two puffs, and was reminded he hadn't eaten in hours. He threw it away. He was so hungry he couldn't smoke, so tired he couldn't see straight, and so busy he couldn't sleep. Ten o'clock. Four hours more.

He shook his head and pushed a button for his next visitor. He jumped as the window behind him crashed to the floor in splinters and a hole a foot across appeared miraculously in the plaster of the wall opposite him. A dum-dum bullet had come through the window, and missed him widely. The Commander dropped below the window level and crawled hurriedly beneath the sill of the broken window. He let out a roar to the men outside his office.

"Who did that?" he demanded.

The Commander had been working on the second floor of an office building in the heart of New York.

Across the street, in a second story window a man was jumping up and down, waving his arm, and heaving a rifle with the other. He paused to direct a bullet at the Commander's window, then continued his performance.

"Bring that man over here!" snapped the Commander. The half-dozen officers and orderlies who had tumbled in, tumbled out, and raced across to the other building. The Commander's personal dignity and personal safety had been touched; also the Commander hoped that anyone firing at him must be connected in some way with the Council of Five.

Three officers returned shortly, bringing the man none too gently. His hair was mussed, his clothes much awry, but he was smiling. He was tall, powerfully built, with a keen intelligent face.

"Hello, Commander. I meet you at last," he grinned.

"Who the hell are you, and what's the idea of trying to snipe me?"

"Oh, you misunderstand me, Commander, I was merely trying to snipe your attention. For the last three hours I have been throwing myself in the way of Major Kendrill, but didn't succeed in seeing him. I tried here for about half an hour, then went across the street and tried that way. I at least attracted your attention."

The Commander glared at him. "What do you want?" he snapped.

The smile disappeared abruptly from the man's face. He was suddenly serious, intent. "Commander, what do you want most right now?"

"Power, damn it, power to run my Harrell tubes," replied the Commander with a groan.

"And that's what I've spent three hours trying to give you. Kendrill didn't have time for me, he was busy talking to some nut who wanted him to use automobile generators for power. He'd never heard of James Atkill, and wouldn't see me, too busy with those nuts. Anyway, how much power do you want?"

The Commander looked at him sharply. "James Atkill. Are you he?"

"Right." The smile was back.

"I want at least four million horsepower."

"Make it five. Can you handle it, if I put it on your lines all in one place?"

"Yes. I think so. Where do you get it...Canada?"

"No. Generate it. Come on, and call Kendrill. I'll demonstrate."

The Commander followed without a word. Three dazed officers watched him go with the lunatic that first shot at him, then made him follow him.

The Commander followed half a block to a public hangar, where a small cabin autogyro was parked in Atkill's name. From it, Atkill, with the aid of two men, took a small, very heavy packing case, and a second box of black bakelite, surmounted by a glass globe, under which burned a flame of steady, unwinking white light. It seemed frozen flame, motionless, undisturbed by position.

"What voltage here?" he demanded of the hangar attendant, indicating the lights.

"One-ten."

Atkill set something, plugged a wire into the wall socket—the lights suddenly blazed up, the lights on the streets winked once, and died instantly. "Fuse blew out. Current going the wrong way now." But the hangar lights still burned.

"What is that?" demanded the Commander.

"This is a Warren atomic generator. Ever hear of 'em?"

"NO—let's see, wasn't Warren that scientist that was blown up by something he was working on?"

"Nope—he was blown up, but he was blown up by our mutual friend Thaddeus Nestor, head of the Council of Five," replied Atkill. "I know. He wanted me to do it for him, and I backed out. Principally because I thought too much of Warren, and too little of Nestor. Warren's a better man than I am, I guess—or was. The man was clever to make this. That thing is patented—the patents are in Washington, and nobody ever took the trouble to investigate them after Warren died, except Nestor. He bought the patents. I'm bootlegging this thing, liable to infringement of the patent laws." Atkill then grinned ingratiatingly. "Goin' to prosecute?"

"*Nestor! Council of Five!* Who the hell are the others?" demanded the Commander.

"Not that that'll do you any good, but the others are William J. Fordham, Arthur Benholt, Thomas Ringman and one 'Burt' Hillen."

"Fordham Benholt and Ringman—the power men. That's why the power plants all went up. They're in on this, eh? But who's Hillen? Never heard of him."

"Huh—probably not. He was a secondary gang leader in New York here. He supplied the men who run the air ships. I stole one of the ships with the aid of Joe Keller and his gang. We had quite a shooting scrap up-state. Nobody made any complaints, so you didn't hear. Our ship is painted with a huge American flag, so don't fire on it when we come. We may be able to help, you know. I would have come to the government sooner, but I'd simply have gotten kicked out for my pains. I had to almost assassinate you before I could see you now.

"If Nestor wins, there will be a Council of Four. Hillen and Company, having served their purpose, will be wiped out by an ingenious little radio-controlled gas arrangement in each ship. We stole the flagship, and found the controls for the device in it. They'll have changed the controls of course, but I'm going to try it when the battle starts, anyway.

"Now if you will show me where you want this power delivered, I'll put the generator in."

"How much power?"

"This, my dear sir, is the energy of annihilated matter. I could produce enough energy with this small machine here to fuse New York State in about ten seconds. I've been too busy with that captured ship—it wasn't finished—to make weapons, but just call for all the power you want."

"Come on. Damn Kendrill. The batteries are in the New York Edison plant, and that's the best distributing point," said the Commander.

Half an hour later a group of men watched Atkill kindle the release-flame on the top of a two-hundred pound block of soft, gray iron. It burned steady and white and cold, and the meters on the wall jumped into life. Direct current he was using, direct current that poured into the giant batteries now, and into the mains that led across the city. A million lights blazed suddenly into life, a thousand trains started throbbing as the electric pumps automatically compressed air into the tanks. A sudden hush came over the city, noise died suddenly. The great mobs that had been struggling, shouting, panic-stricken nearly, were filled with a sudden hope as the familiar, comforting power came back. The meters on the walls rose to undreamt of heights, as toasters, coffee pots, waffle irons, lights, motors, a thousand and one things about the city came to life. And too, the giant batteries were drinking deep of the power-flood.

A group of bewildered engineers stared at a neat black cabinet, a rough, gray mass, and a clear, cold white flame that burned unwinking and unmoving on the block of metal.

"Good heavens, man, how long can that last?" asked the army engineer standing beside Atkill.

"That," replied Atkill with a faint smile, "will last about a century and a half at the present rate of consumption, thanks to the genius of the greatest physicist that ever lived, Randolph Warren. I used to think I was good, but there are things about these generators even I can't see the why of, and though I know there are a thousand other things to learn, I can learn but a few. The field of absolute

198

zero Warren had, I can't find. A field that will extinguish that flame before the fuel runs out Warren had, from some of his statements in the patents, yet I can't find it. But that will last far longer than you will."

The men looked up at the clock by common impulse. It was fifteen minutes of ten o'clock.

"I'll have to go," said Atkill. On the roof of the powerhouse he entered his autogyro and flashed away to the southwest.

The men in the power house looked at the steady white flame, at the meters, and followed Atkill's simple instructions.

"Leave it alone," he had said. "Leave it alone, and draw all the power you need. If I am killed, just draw on it till the fuel is gone, and then the flame will go out automatically. Before that time you cannot change it in the slightest."

And it would be a century and a half before that was gone!

CHAPTER SEVENTEEN

"I THINK, Major Kendrill, that it will be best to communicate with Washington and announce that we have power," said Commander Coache. He winked a very broad wink. Major Kendrill looked puzzled.

"But," he objected, "that will simply mean that the full forces of the Council of Five will be directed against us, instead of having a divided force to fight."

"Certainly, Jack, certainly. That's exactly what I want, you nut." Commander Coache became suddenly Gil Coache, arguing with his old and good friend Jack Kendrill. "We've got power to fight 'em, and they have just nine ships, Atkill said. He will be here to help us. He can't divide his force. Washington has no power, and no defense. We can't battle them here if there is another half of their force hanging over Washington, and announcing that they are going to wipe out that city if we so much as harm one of their machines here. Atkill solemnly assures me they could—and without a second thought they would."

"Right!" agreed the Major.

A few minutes later the most powerful broadcasting station in New York City was sending out its message on twice its usual power.

"Power has been supplied to this city at the last minute! Dr. James Atkill, famous physicist, appeared here shortly before nine, and offered to Commander Coache a new generator of power.

"It was brought in a small autogyro, and is scarcely larger than a good-sized packing box. Yet it is now supplying the entire city with unlimited power. With this sudden, and welcome power, the best defense of the city, the powerful Harrell tubes, become operative.

"Dr. Atkill has left now, to join his men, who have a ship similar to those of the so-called Council of Five, but more powerful, for the scientist has introduced more weapons. It is confidently felt that between the ground forces and the powerful force in the sky, the few ships the Council can bring against us will be destroyed. Dr. Atkill reported also that there were but nine ships in the hands of the enemy, so if the forces are divided between Washington and New York, victory is certain."

Commander Coache chuckled as he heard it over the radio, and eight million other people, in and near New York, sighed with relief as their radios brought them the glad tidings. With the coming of power they were once more in touch with the world, and the world was well!

*　　*　　*

THADDEUS NESTOR scowled blackly at the radio. The ship under his feet heaved slightly as a powerful up-draft rocked even its massive structure. "Well," he queried impatiently, "what shall we do?"

"We can't afford to lose our ships—we can't afford it. If we don't have them, the whole venture is lost. I am sure that ungrateful renegade, Atkill, will have told them who we are," wailed Ringman.

Nestor scowled even more deeply. Fordham looked thoughtful. "I wonder if they'd dare attack our ships over

New York," he suggested, "if the ships over Washington threatened to destroy that city."

Nestor's scowl vanished. Ringman sat up with a look of dawning joy.

"Oh, of course not," he said happily. "We could kill every man and child in the city. They wouldn't dare."

"If they destroy one ship, we'll rip up Pennsylvania Avenue with the heat ray. I think that would stop them. And we can send four ships to New York, and five here, as planned," went on Fordham. "Give the orders, Nestor."

Nestor gave the orders unwillingly. Fordham was taking control, and Nestor didn't like it. However, that was the right idea. There would be no battle in New York, Washington would be the scene of any trouble.

In three minutes the orders had been given, and in another one the ultimatum had been given to New York City and its defenders.

High above the city of New York four slim ships floated. On the side of each metal hull was a patch of bright blue paint, with five silvery stars on it.

Deep under New York City Commander Coache was sitting at his desk, his head in his hands.

"I was afraid of that—but there was nothing else to try. I hoped they wouldn't think of it—but it was too obvious."

Something wailed through the sky like a dart of red and white. High—very high in the air. It seemed pointed with a long nose of light, and the sword of radiance swept suddenly, and struck a shining dirigible of metal squarely amidships. The dirigible of metal exploded with a terrific thunder, yet without a flash of light. The two halves were flung abruptly across the heavens in opposite directions, falling rapidly toward New York City and its crowded populace. Something stopped them, gripped the two halves, and drew them together again, then hurled them with a force inconceivable out toward the open sea. They glowed white-hot, shining brilliantly in the young morning light. Far out at sea they fell with a terrific hiss.

Long before they fell, a second ship had been caught in the grip of that same hurling force, and went flying end over end, out to sea, and down. It struck off Sandy Hook, and was crushed beyond all recognition, driven through thirty fathoms of water, and twenty feet into sand and mud and shattered rock.

But then the other two ships began their work. And the land defense stations, which had been under orders to remain inactive, became very active, as the orders were countermanded.

Reaching fingers, that glowed green in the daylight, reached out toward the fighting, streaking ships—the red-and-white dart of Atkill's ship, covered with an enormous American flag, and the silvery darts of the ships of the Council of Five.

Burt Hillen was commanding one of those ships, and he fought as best he knew how, but what did any of them know of this new fighting at terrific speed, and under terrific acceleration. Atkill's men were strapped and bound at their posts, their hands scarcely capable of movement. They were splinted and bound in position that they might withstand a slightly greater acceleration, and have that extra ten feet of speed per time-unit, that would put them beyond the reaching finger of a ray.

A dozen rays from ground stations reached up at the two silvery ships. But all those rays seemed to flood harmlessly against a shining, shimmering coat of radiance. The ships were protected against those radio waves. So simple—too simple to overlook. They were protected against the heat rays that Atkill lashed at them.

Then one of them was touched, barely touched by the sword of radiance that had struck the first ship. As the beam struck it, the molecules of its metals were suddenly freed of every bond, and the ship became a thing of gas, tremendously compressed gas. It expanded. But it had been touched only, and but one small portion expanded.

Unfortunately, for the officers and crew, this small portion included the control that kept the release-flame within bounds. The men in the control room died instantly as the inconceivable blast of steel molecules struck them. That steel had been under a "pressure" of about a hundred thousand pounds per square inch due to its own molecules. With the release of the terrific pressure it expanded. The expansion destroyed everything in its path.

A man dragged himself along the corridor a moment later. His nose, his ears, his eyes even, were all bleeding. His face was contorted with pain, till Burt Hillen could scarcely be recognized. He stopped as he entered the power room. There was a fierce, unaccustomed heat beating out of its doorway. The man raised his eyes and looked. The white flame had become an angry violet color, and it pulsed slowly, but faster and faster, as he watched it. With each pulse the ship seemed to rise, then fall, rise and fall—the flame grew steadily, the pulsations came more swiftly, and the difference grew greater. The man turned and fled before the heat, but it seemed to pursue him.

Suddenly the ship lurched, then pressed downward. The man was struck by the overhead deck as it descended on him, and he became a rust colored stain on the deck, a stain that was likely a queerly contorted man. In a moment he was gone, for the ship had become a white-hot mass.

Atkill had known that ship was finished. He had turned to the other, pursuing him now, striking at him with rays that leaked through his screens, for their power was as great as his. He turned his beam on it, and a great strip disappeared from the side of the ship. Simultaneously the ship seemed to bulge, cracks appeared in its walls, and its course became erratic.

Then he became aware of the force that was pulling his ship, tugging it to one side, and upward.

"Atty!" called Joe Keller. He pointed up, and to one side. A great ball of white fire was rocketing down, down toward the city. As he watched a violet flame seemed to lick its way through the wall of white flame, and grow swiftly in size.

"Atty—if dat hit's the city, dere won't be nothin' lef' but a lotta puddles o' boilin' water!"

Atkill's face grew white. He could feel now, the pull of that white fire. It was growing, as the violet flame grew larger, and masked the great steel hull, white-hot now.

Atkill's hands worked rapidly at the controls, a plane of force formed under that thing that no matter could penetrate. The white-hot thing stopped, and suddenly, from behind him came a shriek from the power room, the shriek of the over-loaded white flame. Atkill's face went whiter as he saw what the thing on the dial before him was saying.

"Joe—*I can't stop that!*" There was violet flame crawling on the force-plane now, and with all the energy of his white release flame, Atkill strove to damp that force that ate through his shield. He maneuvered directly beneath it; the shields he had used he withdrew, so that more power might go to that plane of force and he began to push toward the open sea.

The ball of death above him was attracting the earth, dust was rising, water seemed flowing into the harbor, a tide that rose quickly, and crawled out over the streets, flooding them with a rapid, silvering tide.

Atkill's hands were steady, his face white under its tan. Keller fell silent. This man, Atkill, almost a god to him, could not handle that thing—he had best keep quiet.

The violet force was eating holes in that plane of force, and here and there a glob of white-hot steel fell through, to hurtle down, and fall into the harbor.

"Where ya goin'?" asked Keller at last.

"Out—to sea—where it can't—do any damage," muttered Atkill.

The holes were widening now, growing larger. The ship and its terrible burden were moving swiftly now, the water whirling behind them, the restless sea was under them soon, but Atkill wanted the deep water beyond the Continental Shelf. He knew that this thing would burn itself out in a month, but in that month the sea about it, and the rock below would be a boiling inferno.

Out—out—out—

"God! The power's droppin!" Atkill's voice was shrill with excitement, horror perhaps.

The shrill whine from the outraged white flame back there was growing in pitch now. But as it grew higher and shriller, the flame itself dwindled, slowly, but then more and more rapidly—the holes in the shield grew—

Watchers on ships reported it. A terrific flash, a roar of thunder—and the great white ball of steel with the violet flame burning over it steadily seemed to swell, then drop at great speed down—down—and the sea rose up in a mighty flash of spouting steam.

There were few ships that lived to report it, and as Atkill had foreseen, it still boiled for a month. And the sea was redolent of dead fish for a thousand miles about.

But the crippled air ship Atkill had left behind as he carried off that deadly white-hot thing lay a smoldering, blistered wreck on Long Island. The Harrell tubes had at last gotten in their energy for the screen had been ruined by Atkill's ray.

It was over in three minutes. Even that last ship had fallen to Long Island inside of that third minute. But in Washington the action had begun.

CHAPTER EIGHTEEN

"THE fools, the blundering, doddering fools! They think we don't mean it—they think we can't. We *will*—we *will!*" Nestor almost shrieked in anger and mad rage.

Through the radio came the excited, terrified voice of "Sparks" Cohen, Burt Hillen's radio operator, "Atkill attacked, he blew up Jimmy's ship somehow—sort of a ray—he threw it clear out to sea with somethin'—I can't—Gawd—there goes Dan's ship now—way out—smashed on Sandy Hook—he's comin' after us—we're dodgin'—they're workin' beams down below now, and—" A terrific crackle of sound from the set announced the first explosion aboard Hillen's ship.

"Get Bell," snapped Fordham. A moment later Bell's radio operator was talking.

"Atty's beam hit us, and damn near blew us up—it's hot as hell—the ground stations frying us with rays. The shields ain't workin' right anymore. Can you get me? The engine's gone blah—it's hot—*Gawd! I'm fryin'!*" The radio went dead.

"They've ruined our ships—four of our ships. They ruined our ships, and by godfry, we'll ruin their city!" Nestor was almost incoherent with rage and disappointment. "And Atkill may be coming here!"

A long beam of green light reached down, and struck the great Washington Monument. The towering finger of stone and metal seemed to puff, glowed green, and slump like melted butter, to run down to the ground, down the gentle slope to the streets. It was not hot, merely liquid, glowing faintly greenish, and gradually the glow died out, and the rock and metal became rock and metal again. But where they passed automobiles, roadside trees, men and women glowed green, slumped, and ran with the stream.

The beam moved, swept across toward Pennsylvania Avenue—and suddenly, it was chopped off in midair, half way to the ground. It simply ceased to exist at that height. It did not reflect and it did not glow. It just ceased to be.

Other beams had started now from the other ships, but like this first from Nestor's flagship, they stopped ineffectually half way. Some sparkled and arched with spitting flame, but none passed that barrier.

Then they looked up, and far, high in the sky was a shining ship, a sixth. It was as long as Nestor's, but thicker, more graceful. And its metal shone with a burnished blue tinge. It sank slowly toward the five ships, and the five beams that reached that impenetrable wall of force were suddenly gone. Twenty beams reached from each of the five ships, and played on the lone ship above. In an instant it was wrapped in blue flame.

"I think," said Warren grimly, "we got back just in time."

"I wish I knew what had happened to Atkill after that last ship went down over New York," replied Putney. "And I think we had better start active work. They may be able to get more power out of their generators. I'm glad you didn't patent that control-field. They haven't got it and have to work their generators at one-fiftieth the load— but they may have them ten times as big, remember."

Warren was silent. Outside a solid sheath of roaring, spitting, blue flame beat at a sheet of pure force, indestructible while their great generator maintained its power. There were some forces that could penetrate it, gravity for one, and a certain peculiar beam that Warren was working with. But no beam that Nestor's men had at their disposal could do it.

"I see that Atkill didn't help them after we left," remarked Warren without taking his eyes off the peculiar view-plate before him. "He'd have learned something perhaps. He's good."

In the view plate appeared the interior of first one and then another of Nestor's little fleet. As though they had been made of the clearest glass, they appeared on the screen with their interiors perfectly exposed.

"Nestor, and the power-boys are in that slightly longer ship. Nestor hasn't been playing square by his boys, I suspect. The other ships all had gas-tanks, as you suggested, only they've been disconnected, as you didn't suggest. Nestor's on the other hand, has one oxygen tank that's full of something that looks suspiciously like tri-nitro-toluene. A bit old-fashioned, but exceedingly effective, I suspect. I should say there was about three hundred pounds of it. That should scatter that ship all over the district." Warren continued to inspect the enemy ships at his leisure. Outside, a hell of fighting energies flamed and flared in the clear, sunlit sky.

"Well—are we ready?" asked Putney, as Warren straightened up.

"Uh-huh," replied Warren laconically. He settled himself in the pilot seat, and pulled a little control. The ship seemed motionless, while Washington shot back with an incredible acceleration, swung away, shot to one side, and snapped back.

Five ships hung in the air, moving slowly toward the mote of the *Prometheus* that hung in the sunlight like some grain of shining dust, and shot about with velocities and accelerations that left the five ships helpless, which were to have subdued a nation.

Without warning, one of the five reversed its direction, and headed out toward open space with a speed and acceleration inconceivable. It seemed to flatten, its length vanished. It was a disc of wreckage resting on some clear plate. Then it contracted upon itself, and vanished, a white-hot point in the heavens. A second ship did not move from its position. But it contracted to a ball, five feet in diameter, and suddenly flamed violently blue. An instant later something wrenched all space, the blue flame disappeared, and with it, the mass of metal that had been a ship was gone.

Three ships remained, and struggled against the *Prometheus*. Like some inconceivable giant planet bombarded with meteors, the *Prometheus* continued unimpeded. Methodically a third ship suddenly contracted as a sphere of pure force closed in on it, flamed blue as its release flame burst its bonds, and snapped into nothingness with a roll of thunder, as the extinguishing field reached it, and killed the atomic fires. And space seemed to be distorted each time, and the sun shifted sharply in the sky, and things seemed out of focus. The terrific space-fields bent the light away.

One ship was left, the longest. It had turned and fled across the city, out across the sea. The *Prometheus* followed it effortlessly, as the men within struggled under the awful weight.

"That's—not—Atkill—" Nestor groaned. "I don't know—who it is—but I can—guess—and I don't—want to—believe it!" His face was deathly white, and he was crumpled in his chair under the same terrible weight, as the ship accelerated madly. It was headed toward the eternal night and eternal glare of space, now.

"That's Warren. I thought he was dead," said Fordham. He was younger, and stronger, the acceleration affected him less.

"So—did I. I wish—he was."

The acceleration of the ship dropped slowly. Men came running from the power room, their eyes covered, crying out in terror. The eternal, inextinguishable flame was dying. It simply contracted, turned a dull gray-white, then to red. The acceleration dropped. Presently there was none, and the ship began to fall to earth. The flame had died, the ship was without power.

"He stopped us." Nestor said it with a baffled wonderment. "He shouldn't stop us. Nothing will put out the Flame. Atkill said that."

"Yes," Fordham said, his voice sounding heavy, "but the only trouble is that Warren is the man who invented that thing, and he's got it trained, it seems." The men were suddenly aware that an acceleration had returned, a weight. "Well, he's at least keeping us from falling. It's about two hundred miles down, and we would have landed rather heavily."

"Why is he taking us, why didn't he just wreck the ship?" whimpered Ringman. His nerve was gone. This morning he had started out, one of the five Rulers of Earth. It wasn't eleven o'clock yet. He was on his way back now, a captive, helpless.

There were milling, calling men back in the ship. They were frightened now, afraid of that ship that could kill the flame that destroyed anything, against which its awful powers were helpless.

"I suspect he's taking us back to turn us over to the government," Fordham said, smiling bitterly. "It was a great plan, Nestor. Only you can't seem to kill that man Warren."

CHAPTER NINETEEN

THE *Prometheus* settled beside the steel hull of the lifeless ship. A mass of infantry advanced rapidly across the great airport, two staff cars raced ahead of them.

"Nestor—Nestor—Nestor—come out of the ship, without weapons. Send your men out one at a time." The radio was useless, as Warren decided after several tries. No doubt the power for it had gone with the extinguishing of the flame.

A beam reached out from the *Prometheus*. It sliced rapidly down across the tail of the lifeless ship. A section ten feet long fell to the ground as a line-thin strip of incandescent metal appeared under the beam. The staff cars were parked some fifty feet ahead of the *Prometheus*, a cordon of infantry had established itself about the two great ships.

Warren stepped out of the *Prometheus*, stamped the short-cropped turf joyfully, and looked up at the tall, imposing officer who bore down on him. Warren grinned happily at him.

"Well—General Walters. I'm pleased to meet you, immensely so. This is the second time. The last time you urged me not to waste your valuable time, I believe. In connection with the release of certain inter-spacial energies, wasn't it?"

"Forgive me, man. I was stupidly wrong. Almost criminally wrong. Had it not been for you, whom everyone thought dead, everyone in this city would have been dead. We heard their orders on our radio sets."

A gray-headed, stooped old man, with tired, lusterless eyes stepped from the steel ship. Three other men followed him immediately, one so broken in nerve and body that another had to almost carry him.

"Thaddeus Nestor, I arrest you for High Treason against your country." General Walters' voice was vibrant with a fury he could scarcely contain. Nestor looked up with his tired, lusterless eyes, and nodded.

*   *   *

WARREN sat back comfortably in the great lounging chair in his New York apartment. "Put, they seem to feel they owe the whole rescue to us." He chuckled slightly. "But I think they ought to say they owe the whole trouble to us. We invented the thing.

"Besides, Atkill saved New York before we even got here. We were still on the outskirts of the atmosphere when he started."

"And now, Atkill is a hero—but a dead one. Cremated with Hillen, but he saved New York. The rays from that thing would have burned every human within a hundred miles, and so badly they probably wouldn't have recovered." Putney rose, and looked out over the city. Far to the east, barely visible over the horizon was the great, glowing cloud of steam, shooting up to the heavens, glowing weirdly in the intense violet light.

"Too bad we couldn't extinguish that," he said ruminatingly.

"I'd be afraid to. Might throw the whole Earth into that other space to extinguish anything that big.

"But Putt, is Atkill cremated in that?"

"Were we blown up? It's impossible to tell from this space." Warren looked at his friend with questioning eyes.

THE END